The Meantime

Nine short stories from Brussels

Edited by Edina Dóci, Nick Jacobs and Monica Westerén

Production and design by Dany G. Zuwen

Contents

Prologue

They arrive on high-speed trains and budget flights. They travel light. They pass through security scanners and station forecourts, flat-share websites and admin offices. They come for work or love or direction; they leave for the same reasons. The city embraces them, but its arms are cast so wide that they cannot feel its pull. They are talkative and tongue-tied, hunted by the ticking clocks in all of their time zones. Nothing constrains their freedom, but is nothing a reason to stay? They must *choose*, over and over again.

☼

Olivier Gbezera

The Lovely Streets
The Story of Him

Under the dark moon the lonely streets all look the same. Too many details follow you, look at you, silently ask you what you are doing out at such an ungodly hour, when everyone else is sound asleep. The silent disapproval is not lost on you, as you walk a little bit faster, think of short cuts, avoid dark alleys.

The streets here are like nowhere else: almost all of them have two names. You can be in one place and say that you are in another, and still be telling the truth. That is one of the many intrigues of bilingualism: ubiquity. The city itself has two names. Or is it three now? Regardless of the language, the dark streets under the lonely moon still see you, follow you, question you. No matter how hard you try to blend in, no matter how fast you walk, no matter how high the volume of your mp3 player. They've seen it all: they were here before you were born. And they were born here, unlike you.

You hum along to a song you've never heard before. You look around, desperately searching for something less overwhelming than your own thoughts. Something, anything, to get your mind off yourself. A sold-out concert featuring a band you've never heard of, movie festivals taking place at the same time, courses to help you eventually, ultimately, maybe-one-day be able to speak both of this city's languages and become ubiquitous yourself. At this, you laugh

3

under your scarf.

The street, in all its compassion, laughs back at you. A man on a poster invites you to a demonstration, but the message is lost in elegant dots and curves. A Polish writer seems to be in town for a conference. For anyone this side of Germany, what the conference is about shall remain unknown.

☼

As you walk further, the street lights merge into one another, and shadows now precede your every step. You look around: hardly any lights are on, and you wonder what the people with lights on are doing. Watching a movie, studying for an exam or a *concours*, reading, kissing, fucking, sleeping with the lights on to stop dark memories and unresolved dilemmas creeping up from under the bed. You scan the windows, trying to read these random lives through them. You think that there might very well be someone you know fucking someone else you know right now, this city is so small after all. Whoever these people are and whatever the reason for their lights being on, they do not know you are walking beneath their windows wondering about it. And they could not care less.

You end up walking for what seems like hours. Your legs start to evaporate under you until you can hardly feel them anymore. You walk like you breathe, automatically and effortlessly, until you have to stop at a light. No car coming either way, so you ignore the red light. You try to trot across, but you feel your legs now, aching and yelling at you as you reach the other side of the street. What time is it anyway? You realise your mp3 player is still playing, but can't figure what you're listening to. You switch it off, and look at the time: 1.15 am.

☼

You know you have to wake up early tomorrow, or rather today: you knew it before going out and still went. You had been trying to have a drink with her for a couple of weeks, but things kept coming up: friends or family visiting, you were out of town, she was out of town, too much work, too tired, too this, too that, too often. You figured that a drink in the middle of the week would not end very late anyway. So out you went, trying hard not to think about your nine o'clock job interview.

☼

She is lovely, as expected. Despite the cold weather and seasonal clothing, her features stick out, stabbing you deep inside. Her skin as soft as a peach, or so you imagine, listening to whatever it is she is saying. When she pauses, you realise she has asked you something, but have no idea what. She smiles, and asks if you want another drink. You smile back, and say Sure. When she gets up, you look at her walking to the bar, and look away as she turns around to look at you looking at her.

It turns out she hasn't been in town for long, and that she has spent most of her time here abroad. She hardly knows the city except for its Irish pubs and main metro stations. The job is very time-consuming and she has to travel a lot, she says, and you nod. The weather sucks, she says, and you nod again. Thank God spring is around the corner, she adds, and she will be travelling less. You smile.

You realise that for the first time in five months you seem to know the city better than somebody else. That gives you confidence. You talk about yourself, about your internship here, about the city. She smiles through it all, discovering it second hand and loving every minute detail. She asks questions about you, and you are surprised by the attention, in part because you hadn't expected it from her, in part because you aren't used to it anymore after five months of chit-chatting at after-work drinks.

So you share more with her over a beer than you have shared with anyone since you got here, with this beautiful girl you're seeing for the second time in your life. She looks deep into your eyes as you talk, and you look as far away from her as you can. You let a question linger and go get two more beers. As you walk to the bar, you do not turn around to see if she's looking at you.

☼

You keep on walking, thinking about your interview, now just a couple of hours away. You try to figure out how you can wake up as late as possible and still be there on time. Luckily, the interview is not too far from home, nor from your internship.

The streets never talk, but you can hear them clearly. Why today? You look around, and spot a car in the distance. The car approaches, strangely silent, its eyes staring at you, getting closer and closer. You stop, and watch as the car nears. It roars as it passes by, waking you up. Inside, a couple: the man looks straight ahead, and as the woman looks at you, you look at her. You can't take your eyes off her, and she doesn't take her eyes off you, turning her head as they drive by. Then, she disappears in the darkness, and the endless second is over. You feel your legs aching.

You hear the question again, why today? Why not, you are tempted to answer, but to whom? And why exactly why not? Your answers become questions, and you feel you will be walking forever.

☼

When she goes to the bar for another round of drinks, you

quickly look at the time. You realise you'll probably miss your last metro home. The place is still quite full, and you guess that some of these guys will be going home with their date, but that most of them won't. You start wondering who is most likely to be walking home alone later on, an impromptu study of the solitary male. You are amused by this, until you realise you have some of the characteristics of those filed under 'walking home alone': anxious foot-tapping, nervous drinking and discussion dangerously approaching friend-territory. You try to shake the impression that you might be right, as she gets back to the table, two beers in hand.

She talks about herself, and she smiles at you constantly. You want to empty your beer, and you want her to empty hers so you can both get out of there. You have no idea where she lives, but know that your place is too far, and you didn't bring enough cash to grab a cab. She mentions she lives nearby, and you start paying attention again. She then starts talking about her house back home, and you take another sip of your beer.

You excuse yourself, go to the toilets, and there, between party flyers and rest-room graffiti, decide you have to make your move if something is to happen tonight. You think that most girls don't just bring guys home on the first night, but then again most girls don't spend four hours drinking beer on the first night to begin with. The signals are mixed, you don't know what to do with them, you only know what you want to do with her. You yawn and look at your watch, horrified: half past midnight.

☼

A bus rolls down the street, and you wonder where the hell it can be going this late. The driver stares straight ahead, looking like he could use a couple of days of sleep. You wonder how long the driver would take to react to a half-drunk pedestrian crossing the road at a red light. You hope no one will find out.

You should be getting there soon, you think. Another car silently creeps up on you, and you only see it as it pulls up next to you. An old man asks you something. You don't understand what he says. You guess he's asking for directions, but cannot make out what he is looking for. You have no idea what he is saying and in what language, as he desperately looks at you. You shrug and mumble Sorry, and he waves you off. As he drives away, you look at the licence plate, a local one. You try to remember why you never took those language courses.

When you get back from the toilets you see that she has gotten up and put her coat on. She says it is getting quite late and that she should get going. She has to get up early tomorrow. You agree and curse at yourself as soon as you say that you too must be up early. She asks at what time, and you answer earlier than usual because of a job interview. She says Great, and asks for what kind of job. You answer for a development NGO. She says Great again, that she hopes it will work out, and you hope she won't ask where the job would be based.

As you get to the door, she asks where the job would be based, and you want to lie but don't, and tell her what you don't want her to hear. The job would be in Latin America you say, in Guatemala. That sounds great, she manages to say, and adds that she hopes it will work out. You hope she doesn't mean it the way you think she does.

You walk her home, which is in the exact opposite direction of yours, and look for a way to get over the awkward silence and get back to the conversation as it was a beer ago, before alarm clocks, job interviews and potential relocations abroad. She pulls her coat tightly around her, and you think that it's not that cold now. It must be a bad sign. You stutter questions and she mumbles one-word answers with a smile she conceals under her scarf. She walks slightly quicker.

You don't make it up to her apartment, of course. She thanks you for the nice evening, and wishes you good luck for tomorrow, or rather today, and forces a laugh. You say there is no need to thank you, and you thank her. She asks if you will manage to get home, and you answer Of course, as if her question were not a rhetorical one. Neither of you speak for slightly too long, and she opens the door and says that you should do this again soon, if you want to. You say Sure, wish her goodnight and watch her go inside and close the door. You turn around, and the streets welcome you back with a cold embrace.

☼

The streets look nothing like those back home. In a way, they are more familiar: they are foreign to you, as you are foreign to them. The candid distance is refreshing: even as you walk them, you remain mutually separated, one merely acknowledging the other's presence. The more you walk them, the less you seem to know them. You have walked down this street dozens of times, yet you are surprised by a huge fish staring down from a building for no apparent reason. What is it looking at? Where is it diving from? Whichever genius painted it must have been out of his mind, probably a good guy. You wonder, has the fish always been there? You would have seen it. Wouldn't you?

☼

You put your mp3 player on, and look at the time: 0.51 am. You hang around until you see the light flick on in what you guess is her apartment, on the second floor. You wonder what she's thinking now, if she regrets not asking you in. Maybe she does. You hope she does. You hope she'll open the window and look out and look for you and call you if she doesn't see you, asking if, after all, you don't want to spend the night at her place, it's so late and she doesn't want you to walk the streets for God knows how long. You start walking, because you do not want her to see you waiting under her window when she'll appear to look for you. You confidently walk away, and keep your cell phone in your hand, ready to pick up her call. The phone does not ring. Right before taking a left, you glance back at her apartment. The lights are off.

A few weeks earlier, this is where you saw her for the first time, walking in front of you. You were in love before you even saw her face, the way she seemed to glide on thin air had something divine about it. Her high heels were not too high, her *tailleur* was deliciously close to being too tight. It was around one o'clock that afternoon, you guessed that she was going back to the office after her lunch break. So were you, and it seemed you were heading in the same direction.

You were, but she crossed the street and stopped at the entrance of the building in front of yours. You did not know what to do, so you did nothing. You stopped in the middle of the pavement, those heading out on their lunch break bumping into you on one side, those coming back bumping into you on the other. Sandwiches and bottled water galore. You looked in her direction, and saw her take a cigarette out of her bag, and look for a lighter. No one else was in sight. You crossed the street. You cross it again now, and look at your watch: 1.40 am.

You finally get home, hardly registering the fact as you walk up your street. Instead, you notice that the light is on in the kitchen. You don't look at your watch. You don't wonder who is in the kitchen doing what, since you will soon find out.

In the kitchen, you find your flatmate, who looks at you looking at him. You wonder what he's doing there; he wonders where you're coming from. He says that he has been studying for an exam and that he couldn't get any sleep, and you realise that you couldn't care less. You don't ask for which exam or when it will be. You tell him you were having a few drinks, without mentioning her, assuming he couldn't care less with whom. He asks you who with, you say with her, he asks how it went, you want to answer Great, realise that you're in your kitchen at 2.05 am talking to your insomniac flatmate, so you settle for OK. He offers you some coffee and you think of saying something about coffee and insomnia. Instead you say No thanks and wish him goodnight, for lack of a better word.

You wake up surprisingly fresh and repeat to yourself that you just have to make it there and you'll be all right. The interview, you reckon, should take no more than forty five minutes, and you count on adrenaline to get you through it. You quickly go take a shower before anyone can beat you to it, then go to the kitchen and see a four-hundred-page brick entitled *Comprehensive Understanding of the European Institutions*. You shove it aside, grab some breakfast, get dressed, and get out of the apartment.

The street welcomes you with a wet yawn, which you return with a sigh. You walk down the road to your metro stop avoiding incoming umbrellas. You wonder how people manage to eat their breakfast, drink their coffee, hold their umbrella, read their newspaper and walk at the same time. As your eyes unexpectedly meet those of a man walking hurriedly, he spills coffee on his suit and almost blinds you in an attempt to salvage his croissant.

There is hardly any more light than six hours ago, as the herd of dark clouds rests on the top of surrounding buildings, glaring down at you. You look around, and wonder where all the faces went, only seeing speeding umbrellas and swinging newspapers. Your thoughts are interrupted by a honking car, then another, and then another. You wonder what's going on. You speed up when you notice that you are crossing at a red light.

You step into the metro station, hustle down the stairs as you hear a train arriving, or leaving, get to your platform, and sit down as your metro rides away. The speakers announce something, but you can't make it out. Your watch reads 8.21 am.

☼

The interview starts out pretty well: the first questions are about your CV, which you've gone over a hundred times. The interviewers are quite easy-going, more so than you had expected. You try hard not to look at the woman on the right, who looks at you as if she knows something you don't. She hardly speaks during the whole interview, so you manage to focus on not focusing on her and her cleavage, and manage not to wonder for too long why the hell she is wearing such a light dress in this weather, surely a ploy to make you fail the interview. You look at her, and she looks away. You look at her cleavage.

You're in cruise control now. Answers flow out of your mouth with such ease and poise that you are impressed by yourself. You straighten up in your chair. The man in the middle looks satisfied, as does the one on his right, and you avoid looking at the woman on your right so you don't know if she looks satisfied or not.

As the man in the middle pours himself some water and asks you if you want some, you suppress a yawn while answering No thank you, and an awkward silence floats around as he drinks his water. You stare at the emptying glass to keep your focus, as alarm bells start to sound from your energy meter. You pinch yourself and silently beg for the man in the middle to ask another question.

He asks you how you see the position as junior assistant within the NGO. You answer that you see it as a position allowing you to bring your experience to the NGO, to learn by doing and to be part of a highly dynamic and motivated team. He asks what you can bring to the team. You answer your experience, energy, commitment, reliability and creativity. He asks you why the NGO, in your view, needs more creativity. You look at the man on his right, who is looking down at his notes, and answer that it may be required if new situations arise and in order to adapt to a fast-changing environment. He asks you if, in your view, the NGO has not been able to adapt itself to changes quickly enough in the past. You swallow your saliva and look at the woman on your right, whose eyes tell you you'd better get this answer right. You answer that to your limited knowledge it hasn't had issues adapting to changes in the past, which explains the NGO's leading position today in the international development market, you mean field, and that creativity was needed to keep it a step ahead. The man in the middle looks satisfied again. He asks you if you are aware that the position is based in a developing country, you answer that yes you are. He asks if you are concerned about living there, and you say no you are not. He asks if you have ever lived in a developing country, you say not yet but that you are looking forward to the opportunity to take part in building a better future and to defend the NGO's interests, you mean values. Last of all, he asks you what should convince them to pick you over the other fourteen candidates lined up outside, what do you have that they do not. You try to think of something smart to say, something that would ice the cake and seal the deal. You suppress another yawn. You think of nothing smart, so you tell the truth, that you do not know, since you do not know what the other fourteen applicants lined up outside have or do not have to offer. What you do know is what you have, and that is experience, energy, commitment, reliability and creativity. You wonder if you have said that already.

The man in the middle rises to his feet, as does the man on his right and the woman on your right, you shake hands, and he says that you can expect a call shortly and wishes you a pleasant day. You thank them, take a last look at the woman who is still smiling as if she knows something that you don't, wonder whether you might have seen her at some party, meeting, bar, or conference, maybe tried to pick her up, maybe she tried to pick you up, but you can't remember. You step out of the room. You don't look at the other fourteen candidates lined up outside as you walk down the corridor. You check your watch: 9.58 am. You switch your cell phone back on, and wait. No messages.

As you step out of the building you realise that the rain has stopped, and as you look at the sky you feel an icy drop on your forehead. You look around, and see the sun hiding between two clouds and three buildings, shyly smiling at you. You feel a lonely ray of sun massaging your temple, and you take it in for a moment. Then a cohort of badge-wearing women and men almost tramples you, and you move away from the entrance.

You have to get to your internship, a twenty minute walk from here. You consider taking the metro, but you figure you'll get there quicker by walking. You are exhausted, but you could use some fresh air.

You walk straight ahead, through the grey streets of the

European quarter. You wonder what part of this city might not be European. Blue skies and golden stars relentlessly wave at you, but fail to hide the glass and steel trees following your every step. You see umbrellas ahead, and look above, the sun now nowhere to be seen, the hungry clouds raucously plotting their next attack. You bump into an umbrella, and excuse yourself to a pair of out-of-rhythm high heels. You feel a drop on your neck.

The headquarters of the development agency where you are finishing your internship look like the headquarters of any corporation. The façade is as impersonal as you are in your dark suit, and you walk through the same door as the employees of the *European Board of Steel Industries* do in their dark suits. Outside it is still raining and it feels cloudy inside. In the elevator, you recognise some of the faces you have been seeing almost every day for the past five months. Some say Hi, some say Hey, most don't say anything. Some frown, probably thinking about important business, holding important documents on their way to important meetings. You frown too, for no reason.

You get out of the elevator, get into your office, and remember you had a meeting scheduled at 11 am. You check your watch: 10.16. You don't remember what the meeting is about. You turn on your computer and check the agenda. You see that there is no meeting scheduled. You ask a colleague about it, he answers Hi, you say Hi, he says There is no meeting, you say Are you sure, he says Of course, you say I'm sure there was one, he says That doesn't mean that there is one, you look at him waiting for your next move, and turn back to your computer.

You spend the morning avoiding your boss, answering emails, suppressing yawns and looking at the clouds outside. You grab a sandwich for lunch, and eat it silently in the kitchen. You avoid chit-chat by reading a newspaper, until the owner of the forgotten newspaper comes to reclaim it. A guy and a girl are eating their sandwiches at the table, they must have arrived not too long ago because you don't remember their faces. They look young, professional, and excited. They must be interns. You look at them, they look at you and ask if you work here. You say No, you mean in a way, you say you're an intern. They say Oh you too, and find it great that you're also an intern. You learn that they both just arrived a couple of days ago. You learn that they both graduated last June, the guy in International Politics and the girl in International Development. You tell them that you too hold a degree in International Politics, they ask if you also graduated last June, you say No, five years ago, they say Ah and ask why the internship now, you answer because after working a couple of years you want to give your career a new direction, they ask When did you start your internship, you say that you're actually almost finished, they say Oh, they ask if you plan on staying in the city, you say you don't know yet. You learn that it is their first experience abroad and they ask you if you want to join them for after-work drinks at the Grand Ol'Ale with some other interns. You say No thanks, throw away the rest of your sandwich and walk to your soon-to-be-somebody-else's computer.

☼

You get back to avoiding your boss, answering emails, suppressing yawns and looking at the clouds outside for the rest of the day. You look at your cell phone, and see that you have received a message from her. Hey how did the intw go? Hope gr8! Off 2 Lisbon 1 week 4 work, cu soon xxx. You smile, and try to find something smart to answer, something showing you are happy she thought about you but not too happy. You start answering, cancel, start again, cancel some more, and think.

Outside, the clouds continue to roam around like a pack of

wolves. From your office you can't see if it's raining, but you bet it is, not that it makes much of a difference. You think of the early spring back home, of the beach, of your unemployed friends waiting for your employed friends to join them after another day of insecure work. A dream flies by, the clouds quickly swallow it.

You look at the unfinished answer on your cell phone. Your heart pounds and you think that you need to get some sleep. You write Hey there! Good I think, thx for asking, answer soon. Enjoy Lisbon, cu! You deliberate over adding xxx, or soon, or soon I hope, that only cu might sound like cu around, which might come across as who knows when and who cares anyway. You ponder what she meant by cu soon xxx exactly. You sigh and send your answer as it is.

A week passes. Your thoughts alternate between her, the job, her smile, the salary, her body, the benefits, her laugh, the language. You realise that everyone says Great when you tell them that you think that the interview went well. The sky is still cloudy, but it's raining less these days. Yesterday you walked home from the Grand Ol'Ale and it was surprisingly warm. The streets smiled at you as you walked by, and you smiled back at the torn faces on the walls. Bikes have suddenly appeared in the streets. You saw the woman from the interview pedalling past you on the concrete. You looked at her not looking at you. You felt like waving, but didn't see the point in doing so.

You think of yesterday at the Grand Ol'Ale and the three guys you had drinks with. Two other interns and a guy on a one-year contract. All educated short-term migrants, commonly called expats. If all goes as well as your respective interviews have supposedly gone, none of you will be here in six months. None will be going to the city or country of their dreams, none will be leaving for the job of a lifetime, none will be joining their loved one, but none of those three doubts the importance of seizing the opportunity when it presents itself. You think about it, try to decide how you feel about this seizing-opportunities-when-they-present-themselves business. You can't, and look on as the thought wanders off.

☼

You lie on your bed, staring at the ceiling, with your cell phone in hand. She must be back in town by now, but you don't want to seem desperate by sending her a message. But sending her a message would show that you're thinking about her, which is good you guess. You can't make up your mind.

You look at the time: 7.56 pm. You wonder how to fill your Wednesday evening, and have a look at the Babelian pile of flyers next to your bed. A movie would be nice, but too many good ones are playing and you can't settle on one. A play would be nice too, but you wouldn't understand a word. One flyer mentions a free concert in some bar in the centre. Some good music and a beer could work miracles, and you go through your contacts on your cell phone to see who you could go with. You rule out people you met at your internship, your flatmates, your football team-mates, girls you have slept with, girls you wanted to sleep with, girls who wanted to sleep with you, people who must have left by now, people you don't remember, your family, your landlord and people you just wouldn't know what to talk about with. You are left with one phone number: hers.

☼

You lie on your bed, staring at the ceiling, with your cell phone in hand. They must have taken a decision by now, but you don't want to seem desperate by calling them. But calling them would show that you really want the job, which is good you guess. You can't make up your mind.

You can't call them now anyway, so you try not to think about it. You look at your watch: 8.12 pm. The evening promises to move as slowly as grey elephants in the sky. You think about the job, get out of bed and sit at your desk, open the job description on your computer, read it, envision yourself there, and feel a twitch of excitement. A twitch, a far cry from all the jumping up and down when you got the interview a couple of weeks ago. You open your Facebook account, see that she has added you as a friend, take a deep breath and catch your heart as it jumps out of your torso. You deactivate the chat, and accept her invitation. You go on her profile, go through some of her pictures, and marvel at the smiling technology. You send her a message before your brain can stop you. Hey there how was Lisbon? Let me know if you want to do something this weekend, cu soon. You feel like you've just run the marathon. You decide to skip the free concert downtown.

☼

At work the next day, you receive the phone call. It is the NGO. You think you recognise the voice of the man in the middle, who asks if he is disturbing you, you say No, just a second. You get out of your chair and silently run to the corridor. You say Yes, he says that they were very impressed by your CV and your interview and that after some discussion and internal evaluation they would like to offer you the position. You think nothing and say Great and that you are very happy and you ask what the next steps are. He says they will send you an electronic version of the contract and more information about your tasks, and that you can take a couple of days to think it over because This is quite a big step you know. You say Thank you and that yes you know, and that you are looking forward to receiving those documents and that you will get back to them ASAP. He says Great and that he'll be looking forward to hearing from you, and wishes you a good day. You wish him a good day too, and hang up. You stand in the corridor wondering what just happened, look around and recognise nothing. You look at your watch: 4.45 pm. You call it a day.

☼

You walk out of the office, not knowing what to expect next. You knew the interview had gone well, you knew you wanted the job, but you didn't expect you would actually get it. Give it a try, you thought, give it a shot. Why not, you never know, and still don't.

You decide to walk home to avoid the restlessness of the metro. You need some time with yourself, with the streets, with these familiar strangers. You think that walking will help you weigh up your options, help you digest the news that they want you for a job you're not sure you still want. You think that it may be better not to think and you listen to what the cars, the buses and the all-seeing helicopters are trying to tell you. You know them all quite well, but still don't know their language. So you dig into your pocket, take out your headphones and turn on your mp3 player.

You walk down the streets, looking around for answers. The streets' many faces are sending you mixed signals, an old woman needing a facelift smiling at you here, a too-serious-to-be-trusted candidate from the last elections frowning at you and your issues there. You look ahead, and see umbrellas fiercely marching towards you, faceless swords with no pity for your woes. You had not noticed that it was raining. You do not open your umbrella because you forgot it at the office. You hope the tumbling skies will wash away your questions. Your questions seem to bloom.

The plan was two-fold. Plan A was to apply for the job, and see. Plan B was to get a part-time job in a bar whose owner you know, follow some language courses, and wait for the departure of one of the supervisors at the office so you can replace him. A position tailor-made for you, according to the outgoing supervisor himself. Plan B seemed more reliable than Plan A, which is the point of a back-up plan you guess. You wonder what sense that makes.

Now, the plan is looking at you, smiling at you, laughing at you. You wonder what's so funny, you would love to laugh along, you haven't had a good laugh for some time. You think about it as a bony Chihuahua barks at you, and you laugh out loud at the umbrella holding its fancy leash. You feel better. You almost feel as good as you did one week ago, when you were sharing laughs with her at the bar. You wonder what her plans A and B might be. You wonder if she plans to see you soon.

☼

You get home and are greeted by your insomniac flatmate lying on the couch, his face hidden by his four-hundred-page cushion. You guess that he really mustn't have gotten much sleep the last few nights to be able to sleep with the music on so loud. You wonder where the loud music is coming from, and you guess that your aspiring-DJ flatmate is back in town. You walk to his room, and knock on his door. Nothing happens, so you knock harder. He does not open the door, but turns the volume down. Fair enough.

You turn your computer on, check your emails, and see that she has answered you. Great thx kind of tiring but still nice ... how about a drink this evening around 9? You smile and look at the time: 5.41 pm. You answer right away Great, same place as last time?

Then you decide to send her a text instead, not knowing if she will check her emails. You write Hey a drink tonight sounds good same place as last time, at 9?

You lie on your bed, staring at the ceiling, with your cell phone in hand. You try to relax and not to think about the job, and think about Plan B. You think that you should call the bar owner that you know, just to see if he could still work something out for you. You call him, and after a few rings he answers. Hey there, long time no speak! he says, and you answer Hey how are you? He says Great, he asks What about you, you say Great too, and he says Great, and asks So what have you been up to? You say the same old, the internship is ending and you're thinking about what to do next. He says OK so are you staying or going and you answer that you're thinking about it and you hear a beep indicating a message and you think shit I hope she didn't try to call me and there is a silence as he waits for an answer to the question you didn't hear him ask. You say What did you say and he says that he was asking what your plans were and you answer that you don't know, that you got the job but you're not sure about it anymore, he asks Why, you say you don't know, he says I see, you say Yeah, he says anyway if you want to drop by for a drink it's on him and that if you stay you have a job waiting for you at the bar. He adds the job is probably less fancy, but comes with free alcohol, and laughs. You laugh too, and say Thanks man, and that you'll drop by one of these days. He says No worries, and see you soon then! You hang up and look at the text she sent you: 9 o'clock is good, cu there xxx.

You take the metro to get to the bar and decide to get out one stop early. You want to relax by walking. You feel nervous, even more nervous than a week ago. You feel like she will be expecting something to happen, or maybe she might feel that you are expecting something to happen, which may make her nervous. You do not know what you want to happen, you know she will ask you about the job, you will say you got it, she will say Great, she will notice you not being overly enthusiastic about it, she will ask Are you having second thoughts about it, you will say Kind of, she will ask Why, you will lie by saying that you don't really know, or you will open up and share your fears and hopes with this beautiful girl who you will be seeing for the third time in your life.

As you step out of the metro you see a couple on a bench totally oblivious to the fact that their train is leaving. You see a homeless man talking to his dog, who barks back in agreement. A lonely woman looks around for potential threats. Further down you see four teenagers breakdancing to the classical music playing in the station. You do not see the man who almost knocks you to the floor until he almost knocks you to the floor, running after his metro which has just left. He says something to you, but you don't hear him because of the metro storming away. The dog barks indignantly at him, and he sits down on a bench.

The night is warm, you feel good walking down the street under shy stars and loquacious trees, a breeze the only hint of it being March. The pavement feels light under your shoes, and you smile at the bar appearing up ahead. As you get closer, you see her sitting inside, looking around. Your eyes meet: for a second, the world disappears in her irises, your thoughts evaporate in her smile, your questions bow to her presence. You manage to grab the handle before crashing into the door.

☼

You take a deep breath as you enter the bar, your heart drilling through your chest. She stands up to greet you, and you manage to look at her forehead, successfully avoiding her eyes, mouth, breasts, hands, legs, curves and other lovely features. You feel a drip of sweat rolling down your spine. She says Hey there how are you and you manage to mumble Great how are you before collapsing into your chair. She says I'm OK as if she really meant it. She adds Lisbon was great but a lot of work, so she slept the whole afternoon, and she laughs, and you laugh with her. You wonder how many opportunities she did not seize by sleeping the whole afternoon. She says she was supposed to work on a big project this afternoon but that would just have to wait, and she laughs again. You laugh again too.

She asks you So, what about the job? And you answer Yeah well they called me back and they told me I got it, but I'm thinking about it now. She says Are you having second thoughts? You answer Kind of, because you're not sure after all about the job, and about living there right now. She says Oh where do you want to go? You answer Nowhere, I might actually want to stay here for some time and see how things work out. She says nothing, takes a sip of her beer, and says Join the club, because she just refused a job back home, and will be staying here longer than expected. You ask what kind of job and she says the well-paid and not interesting kind, and laughs. She adds that she hesitated about it, but then decided she also wants to stick around, to see how things work out. You smile at her smiling at you and at the unseen smiles floating around both of you.

☼

After the second round of beers and some chat about your family and hers, you ask her if she wants another drink and she says Maybe not, and you say you neither and get up. She gets up too, and you say that you will walk her home, if she doesn't mind, and she smiles thanks.

THE LOVELY STREETS

Outside, the night is still warm, the stars still shy and the trees less loquacious. You say It's a lovely night and she says that's what she was about to say. She smiles at you. You walk slowly, taking in the appeasing calm of the streets, its many faces standing in the shadows, trying hard not to intrude. You smile at them. The moon smiles back at you like a one-headed coin.

Suddenly, nothing happens. No car drives by, no one walks by, no siren wails in the distance. You look around you and see the streets, the whole streets and nothing but the streets, silently comforting you. You feel at ease. Your questions, gone. Your hesitation, vanished. You wonder what you were wondering about in the first place. You get to her place, and she opens the door. She says nothing, and you say nothing too. You smile at her shyly smiling at you as she lets you in. You step inside, look back out, and whisper good night to the lonely streets.

☼

Edina Dóci

Bear Dance

The story of Sonia

– *We are running out of berries! One of us will have to leave to find berries.*

– *We can't leave the forest. If we run out of berries, we can eat moss, we can eat leaves, we can eat bird eggs and nestlings, we can eat mud, or whatever we find. I would rather eat mud than leave our forest. Here we can take care of each other. Outside they stick chewing gum on our fur, they slip steel wire into our cookies, they chop off our heads and hang them on their living room walls.*

– *No, we won't leave the forest! Let's dance!*

– *I can't move. I dread the hunters and the zookeepers and the evil children with chewing gum and wire-cookies.*

– *There are no such creatures in our forest.*

– *They are waiting for us outside.*

– *But we don't have to leave the forest.*

– *We have to, we have to! We are running out of berries. And I'm afraid of the hunters! Would you come out there with me?*

– *I can't. Either you go, or I do, but we can't do it together. There are things we can't do together, and there are things we can.*

– *Like what?*

– *We can dance.*

– I want to crawl around and sing the bear song.

– We can do that too.

– And I want to throw berries at each other.

– We can do that too.

– And I want to make love.

– No, we can't do that.

– Why can't we make love if we can dance and crawl around and sing the bear song and throw berries at each other?

– Little bears don't make love. They dance and play and comfort each other when they feel down. They move like bears and speak like bears. That's what makes them little bears. Little bears don't make love.

☼

I'm sitting on the balcony of our flat, drinking mango juice and drawing bears on a notepad. It's Saturday, the second day of the long weekend that Simon and I decided to spend together without travelling anywhere. It's almost eight o'clock, the twenty-third of the seventy hours of togetherness that we signed up for, to celebrate us, ourselves, our commitment and resilience, our vow: this is our sixth anniversary.

It's early in the morning, but already pleasantly warm. I'm noting down possible topics we could discuss today. I will ask Simon about his best friend, who had a nervous breakdown recently. I like to hear about people with mental problems. I also like to talk to them. If something has broken in the machine you can try to fix it. Simon is always fine, unfailingly stable, like a Swiss watch. It's difficult to get into long conversations with a Swiss watch. 'How are you?' 'I'm fine, thanks.' 'Do you want to talk about it?' 'Tick tock. Tick tock.' Sometimes I wish he had collapsed, I wish his mother had died or he had been fired from his job, I wish he had been molested by his father when he was a child. I'm good at solving problems, comforting people.

What else can we discuss?

My friend's divorce after seven months of marriage. The risk of civil war in Venezuela. The relevance of Marx's crisis theory. That must be enough for today. I can't let another silent day go by.

☼

I take a shower, epilate my legs, armpits, everything, and soothe my skin with baby oil. I put on sexy underwear. I look in the mirror. I look away. I go back to the bedroom and lie down next to Simon. I feel foreign in this tulle lingerie, a bear dressed up as a ballerina.

As my eyes adapt to the shutter-induced half-light, Simon's features, softened by sleep, trace themselves out against the dim bedclothes. It is *he* who chose these impossibly dark, green covers, so that they were in harmony with the smoke-coloured walls that *he* painted, under the photos of moments of happiness *he* has partaken in. It's like I didn't change a thing since I moved in, didn't hang one photo on the wall, as if Simon were the first person I had ever met. It is *his* elegant friends, *his* Simon-featured family members, who cheerfully intrude upon our intimacy.

Simon wakes up for a second, blinks at me and then closes his eyes again. He must have seen that I'm wearing this costume. I'm already disappointed. According to the screenplay, now I would go and change back into a pair of old lounge pants, feel rejected and sit on the sofa all day long, noiselessly hurt. But I don't want to behave according to the screenplay.

Screw you, Simon. I wanted to seduce you, but you don't want to be seduced. Fair enough. What do I care.

You can't do much to avoid the screenplay.

And the thing is that I do care. I'm not in the mood to seduce him

29

at all, but I desperately wish I was still able to.

I touch him. He is hard, but I know that it's just the morning erection, it has nothing to do with me. We have sex once a week, this is our unspoken agreement. We do it in order to keep up the pretence that what we have is a relationship between a man and a woman. He wakes up and touches me. It feels ticklish, but I know that if I laugh, it will kill everything. I resist the urge to push his hand away.

☼

The marginal excitement of the moment when he enters me disappears quickly. He is numb. I'm tired of his noiselessness. I want noises, I want words of excitement, I want shouts, I want to hear his pleasure. I close my eyes and set my imagination free. I'm making love with other men, unknown, rough, violent men. I'm under their control, I'm powerless, possessed, narcotised, bound.

I come. I don't scream, there is nothing to scream about. I just tell him: 'I came'. Now it's his turn. He speeds up.

We change positions, he wants me to be on top of him. I'm not motivated, especially now that I've come. After two minutes I give up, my muscles are tired. I'm a lazy P.E. student. I don't want to run, teacher, I don't want to climb the rope, I don't want to play basketball. Leave me alone, teacher, let me read my book hiding in the closet of the changing room. I'm ill, teacher, I'm a cripple, I have a weak heart, I have a medical certificate, I can't take part in the game. I'm lying on Simon and I let him move.

We shift again, he climbs back on top. I'm getting dry. It's taking too long for him to come. He might also be thinking about other women while he is making love to me. I'm wondering if he sees imaginary women, or women he knows. Suddenly I'm overcome by a burst of jealousy, something I haven't felt for quite a while. I feel a strong impulse to stop him and ask: '*Who* are you fucking right now?'

Ten, fifteen minutes might have passed already since I came. I'm exhausted. I'm searching for signs of his imminent orgasm. I feel exploited, like a body being used for masturbation, although I know how unfair I'm being. Finally, he comes. It's like a shrug, nothing more.

He is still inside me when he asks:

'And what would Soncha like to do today?' The cooing tone is overly familiar, but it sounds alien now, distant, as if he were speaking under water.

I swallow the word 'nothing'. I abort the irritated sigh. I caress his head.

'Whatever you want, sweetie,' I say.

☼

A massive, ginger cat appears on the roof of the neighbouring house; it looks at me and meows inaudibly.

'I don't want to do it,' Simon says. He is playing with a dumpling of silver foil, throwing it from one hand to the other. We are sitting on the balcony, surrounded by the ruins of our breakfast.

'What do you mean you don't want to do it?'

'I mean that I don't want to do it.'

'But you just said that you *did* want to do it,' I remind him. My eyes are following the cat as it paces across the roof in a frenzy.

'You were driving at it with all your questions, so in the end I told you. It crosses my mind, you know, from time to time, but that doesn't mean that I *want* to do it.'

'Why not?' I ask him absently. As his voice gets nervous, mine becomes calmer: a reflex from my childhood that I learned while arguing with my brother.

'Because having fantasies doesn't necessarily mean that you want to … that you've gotta act them out,' Simon says, squeezing the silver foil dumpling. 'I do *imagine* these things but that doesn't mean that in real life I would *do* them.'

'That's irrational,' I say, and light a cigarette.

The cat is tapping on an attic window with its paw. The window opens, and the house swallows the animal.

'I wish you'd never started this conversation,' Simon says.

He stands up, leans on the balcony railing and throws the dumpling onto the street. He's wearing nothing but black underpants and sunglasses on top of his head, and for a moment I see him the way other women would see him, women who haven't been seeing him almost every day for the last six years. Suddenly I can clearly see, almost feel, his tanned skin, his thick, auburn hair, his exquisitely shaped back, his manliness, his beauty. I savour the moment, I know how quickly it will fade away. Before turning back to me, Simon pulls the sunglasses back down, to cover the distance in his eyes, or to feel unbreakable?

He returns to his plastic chair, a chair that we picked up from the street once, long ago, at the apex of a drunken night. The back of it reads 'Lipton Ice Tea', and the front says: 'Don't knock it 'til you've tried it!'. It's yellow and red, it's dreadful. I stub out the barely-smoked cigarette, it doesn't taste good. When did it ever taste good?

'Sonia,' Simon says. 'Come here.'

I get up and squeeze myself between the pieces of eclectic garden furniture that populate our small balcony.

Simon sits me on his lap.

'I don't want to do it, OK?' he says.

He is lying, I know. It feels good.

'Why not?'

'Because of you.'

'But I wouldn't mind.'

'Let's forget about this, all right?' he says. '*You* are my girl. My little bear girl.'

Comforted by his baby talk, I relax and wonder who the hell we are for each other. And I wonder who I would be without him. Maybe I would be a world-famous ballerina by now. But I don't think so; I was never really good at dancing.

☼

I wish I could be on the balcony in my bathrobe all day long, drawing bears on my notepad. I'm not in the mood to explore Brussels' hidden beauties after having managed to ignore them for the seven years I've been living here. I'm six years old now, I want to make the bored face, I want to complain endlessly. I'm hungry, I'm tired. I have to pee, I wanna go home, my legs hurt. I don't have legs at all, carry me!

Silence.

'How's Tom?'

'He's fine.'

'He had a nervous breakdown.'

'Right.'

'So?'

'He's fine.'

'How's that possible?'

'He wasn't doing so good but he pulled himself together.'

'Did you talk to him or do you just *think* he's fine?'

'Yeah.'

'Yeah what? Yeah you talked to him or –'

'I talked to him.'

'And?'

'And he said he was fine.'

'That's all he said?'

'We were on the phone. He's not really a phone person anyway.'

'A phone person? What does that mean, a phone person?'

Silence.

☼

'What do you think about the risk of civil war in Venezuela?'

'About *what*?'

'The risk of civil war in Venezuela.'

'What is it with you today, baby? What kind of a question is that?'

'What do you think about it?'

'Nothing! Jesus.'

'You must think *something*.'

'What is it with you, Sonia?'

'Why? Is it an abnormal thing to ask something interesting, to initiate a conversation?'

'No, but it's totally out of context!'

'What context? What context is it out of?'

'I don't know … the context we're in.'

'There is no context.'

'What?'

'There is no context. There is nothing to be *in* or *out* of.'

'What are you talking about?'

I don't say that we are silent most of the time. I don't say that we don't talk, we don't laugh, we hardly fuck. I don't say that *we* are out of context.

I say,

'I don't know.'

Silence.

☼

I decide not to ask him about Marx's crisis theory. We stop at the Palais de Justice to check out the view of the pallid city for the thousandth time. The vapour of the perspiring asphalt fills my nostrils, it fills me with the smell of summer. There is an old, beige-coloured couple in the square beside us. They look too healthy for their age, they move too gracefully, their skin, their hair, their laughter tell of a lifetime of good nutrition, good habits, money. They are smiling at us, they are talking about us, they are talking to us.

'Ils sont en vacances,' the old man says, 'ce sont des touristes'.

'Ils sont en lune de miel,' the old woman says.

They don't need any reaction from us to maintain the conversation. We are the roofs and the benches for them, we are the view, we are their old car and the songs on the radio from the fifties.

'We were in Tunisia on our honeymoon fifty five years ago!' The old man says. He speaks fluent English, his accent is surprisingly gentle, almost imperceptible.

'I got pregnant there with our first child,' the old woman says and winks, as if telling a mischievous joke. 'What about you? Are you planning on having babies?'

I avoid looking at her. I'm staring at the Atomium in the distance, at this inept, left-behind Christmas ornament shimmering in the smoggy heat. What about you, I want to ask back. She must be at least eighty. I'm angry with her for her kindness, for her happiness. I want to ask her if she smells old in bed.

'I lost our baby a couple of months ago,' I lie finally, talking to the Atomium.

'How sad!' says the old lady, and what's worse, she means it.

'I didn't want to keep it, but he's deeply religious you know,' I'm nodding at Simon, 'and he's against abortion. So in the end I did it with a knitting needle.'

To illustrate, I imitate a knitting movement with my hands.

35

I loathe myself right away. The old couple look puzzled. They stop talking to us. They prefer the roofs and the benches. Simon sighs and refuses to look at me, which means I went too far, and he is right, I *did* go too far but I couldn't stand the envy of these old folks. I couldn't leave them with the illusion that we are a harmonious young couple primed for admiration. We are older in our love than they are. In all honesty, I didn't need a knitting needle to kill our child; it died before it was conceived. Its name was Baloo.

We are sitting in the garden of a bar in Saint-Gilles, surrounded by relaxing lobbyists and well-to-do revolutionaries. The pretty waitress appears from time to time to flirt with Simon, Simon is flirting with the pretty waitress. I'm doing my best to look apathetic.

A group of early-middle-aged people are camped out at the neighbouring table, surrounded by good-tempered dogs and oversized instruments. A woman with a sexless aura is holding a feather in front of her face. She is the only one who speaks; holding the quill must give her this right. While she talks the others are staring at the feather, hypnotised, ready to grab it out of her hand the moment she pauses for breath. Simon is reading a newspaper and I'm gazing at a magazine, to not look ignored, left aside.

I'm listening to the odd people, stealing glances at them. There is a rebel at their table, younger than the others, fresh-faced, hasty, who dares to interrupt the sexless woman, *'I think this talking with the feather is stupid, I like spontaneous conversation ...'* I expect such recklessness to be punished, corrected. *'Spontaneity is the right to interrupt anyone, anytime,'* the woman utters, looking at her comrades, expecting support. *'No, it's just if I have something little to say I want to say it.'* The comrades hesitate for a few moments, and then the mocking starts: '*You saying something little, come on man, you never say anything little ...*'

'Are you satisfied with the wine?' the waitress asks.

'Absolutely,' Simon says, his voice deeper now than when he talks to me. 'You were right to recommend it.'

'Happy to hear that,' the waitress smiles. Her honey-brown eyes are shining like miniature sun-disks. She's not shy, she's not cautious. She makes the most out of her job, her youth, in the form of lustful glances and compliments – they keep her going.

'Are you all right?' Simon turns to me when the waitress is gone.

'Sure,' I say, and compel my facial muscles into a stiff smile.

Simon is twirling a coin on the wood, a shiny coin that someone left on our table, most likely to reward the honey-eyed waitress.

'Did I say something wrong?' Simon asks.

'Of course not.'

'OK,' he says. 'Whatever.'

He turns back to his newspaper and I turn back to the people at the neighbouring table. Meanwhile the fragile harmony of their feather society has broken, there is anarchy and decline, everyone speaks at the same time.

'She's pretty,' I say, tipping my head in the direction of the waitress. 'Don't you think?'

Simon looks up, just in time to catch the eye of the waitress.

'Very,' he says.

'She would be a good candidate.'

'For what?'

'Come on, you know what for.'

Simon is still playing with the shiny coin. I hold out my hand, asking for the coin, and he places it on my palm absently. He looks detached and all of a sudden he looks old too.

'What is it?' I ask.

'I don't know,' he says and shrugs.

'What is it that you don't know?' I'm trying to set the coin spinning but I fail repeatedly.

'I don't know what to do.'

'With what?'

'I don't know.'

'With your life?'

He is sitting motionless, his arms pulled tightly across his chest.

'You don't know what you want to be when you grow up?' I ask.

Simon is looking in my direction, he is looking through me. I go on, hoping that I can chatter the lack of expression off his face.

'I'm gonna help you figure it out,' I say. 'If it's heads, you should be a policeman. If it's tails, then you should be a policy officer.'

I toss the coin into the air, catch it, place it on the back of my left hand and hide it with my right palm.

'I think it's tails. What do you think?' I ask, but Simon ignores my question.

He is hugging himself tight, as if afraid that by letting go he will fall from his chair.

'What's wrong?' I ask him again.

'This,' he says and shrugs.

'What? What do you mean by *this*?'

'I don't know. I'm not feeling good, that's all.'

'Why?'

'I don't know.'

'But why?' I insist.

'Maybe it's Brussels. Or I don't know.' He looks away. 'This weekend. This week, this … this year. The way we are together.'

My heart shrinks to the size of a berry.

'Let's go home,' I say, hurriedly, 'We've gotta do the laundry'.

He frowns; he's still looking elsewhere, nowhere, really.

'I don't have clean socks for tomorrow,' I add, as justification.

It is now justified, we are going home. He takes out his wallet, and puts money on the table.

'Let me finish this first,' he says and pours the rest of the wine from the bottle into his glass.

I watch him drinking, sip by sip. Does he hope that if he sips slowly enough, time will stop and he will never have to look into my eyes again?

'I'll pay at the bar,' I say. I stand up and walk towards the waitress. She is flirting with me, gently, out of courtesy, to show that her prior coquettishness had nothing to do with my property, that her sexual vibes are like the love of Christ, dispensed equally to all. I appreciate her gesture, I'm flirting back and soon I find myself under her charm, the charm of her frank vanity, her confidence, her self-love. I ask her if she wants to have a drink with us, at our place, after she finishes work. She laughs, she's flattered, she doesn't blush. I do.

'What were you talking about?' Simon asks when I'm back at the table. He can't believe it when I tell him, on the metro he's angry, as we get off at Madou he's silent, but, by the time we arrive home, he gives in.

☼

She is getting naked in our bedroom. She is dancing for us, enjoying our attention. Her movements generate soft waves of air, her unfamiliar particles fill the space. Only the small, sci-fi lamp next to the bed is on. Its pale light gives the room the quality of a black-and-white photograph. The dimness of the walls for once feels comforting, and for a moment I consider switching off the lamp, and letting the scene disappear into the darkness.

She invites me to dance with her.

'No,' I say.

'You can't dance?' she asks kindly.

Of course I can dance. Every bear can dance.

'No,' I say.

I watch them making out. I'm getting excited and it makes me feel filthy, and makes me want to hurt someone. But I control myself. I started the joke. Now I have to play along with it until the end. I will not ask them to stop, I will not ask them to play basketball instead. I approach them and kiss the woman's neck. I touch her and let her touch me.

I close my eyes and let myself disappear in my wet solitude.

I open my eyes. Simon is holding my wrist and squeezing it.

'Stop,' he says.

'Why?' I ask him. I stop gratefully.

He is shaking his head over and over.

'What the fuck are we doing?'

'Baby –'

'No, no, just tell me what we're doing!'

'I'm sorry!'

'I don't know what we're … doing with each other.'

I see tears in his eyes.

Now I'm terrified.

Simon never cries. There must be grief if he does.

He covers his face with his hands. I want to hug him, but in the company of this woman I can't. I place my hand on his shoulder. My hand is shaking. The whole room is shaking.

I'm losing Simon.

It's happening now.

The waitress is staring at us; suddenly she looks terribly naked.

'Go, leave,' I say to her.

She doesn't move, just gazes at us paralysed, frozen teardrops on her petrified face.

'I'm sorry,' I say.

The curse is over; she gets back to life, collects her clothes, dresses and disappears.

'Simon,' I say. 'Simon.'

'I'm leaving, I'm gonna go back to London,' he says. His eyes are now hollow and dry. 'I'll move out of the flat by next weekend.'

What can I say?

Simon doesn't want my sympathy, my empathy, and I don't want his. If that's all we can give each other, it's better to give nothing.

Is it better?

Is it?

I say nothing.

I curl up on the bed, close my eyes and hide in the dark. When I come back out, I'm alone. The absence of Simon kicks me in the stomach, my teeth clack on my tongue, the pain calls for tears. Taste of wire in my mouth.

Afredo Zucchi

Thousand Hidden Spirits

The story of Josep

I

'Wanna play some chess *mon ami*? Please, sit down, have a beer, it's on me.'

That's how I met the guy who has become my sort of therapist: Wednesday night, the nineteenth century bar close to Flagey. First come first served – chance picked him up for me.

He sits, places the pieces carefully on the chessboard. Then he addresses me: 'I don't feel like playing chess anymore; shall we get out of this place? I don't feel like talking either, not here. Let's go over there, to the ponds.' He listens to me; I offer him my dreams, truly, and some hash. That's the deal from the very beginning.

We get some beers and rolling paper in a night shop close to the bar. It smells so freakish inside it's impossible to dislike it.

Then, lying on the grass, lights going out, I go first:

'I started smoking hashish by mistake – a girl I went out with, her weird friends. I really didn't before; but I'm getting addicted now. I feel deeper.'

'I see *mon ami*,' he says. 'I feel *Brahma* too.'

'Lately I've been dreaming a lot. It's never happened before.

43

Vivid figures stuck in my mind. A dancing princess: her head in her right hand, severed, no blood. She's pointing to a little white hole in the black wall. I keep trying to get into it, no way. Music doesn't stop. My frustrated efforts are of no concern to the audience: they all look delighted and applaud as if I had succeeded. My efforts feed them. They look confident and serene.'

'Keep going please.'

'What would you do if all of your tracks suddenly got erased?'

'You know there's not much you can do but look into the breakpoint,' he replies.

I was so relieved to have met this guy – only a few hours later did I happen to ask him who he was, where he was from, why he was talking to me. Details.

☼

Marc, my sort of therapist, is half African. That's all I know about him, and that's enough for now.

We've met again, this time in a different place, the city centre. In some ways it reminds me of Barcelona: little streets and bars; alcohol and piss evaporating from the ground.

'I worked here in Brussels for a long year, for a Spanish newspaper, *El Mundo*.'

'Ah,' he interrupts me, 'the big right wing one, isn't it?'

'Exactly. Left, right - who cares ...'

'It's only work, right?'

I nod my head in agreement and give him something to roll - Indian hash, black as the deep sea.

'Only. When I was told I got that job it sounded great - reporter on European Affairs - but I didn't feel any better. My mother knew a guy there, I knew I was going to get it. I was a bit excited, sure, but nothing more. Plus my family was really pushing me to take this opportunity.

By my family, I mean my parents and me. The rest are either gone or don't matter. Before leaving my parents I was, you know, the only child, the little prince. When I finally got my independence, those last two years I spent in Barcelona, things were different.'

'Look at my family *now*, Marc.' I retrieve a picture from my wallet, from a year and a half ago. 'My parents are divorced, but happy. Their smiles are not false anymore, they love me. Each in their own way. My mother? A mix of Margaret Thatcher and Lady D. Her complex of frustrated ambitions weighs so heavily on me: *be the worth of anyone* is her motto, in my bedroom. She married my father because of his status. Very upper class, I can tell you. He's something of an artist though.'

'Look at him,' I continue. 'When the audience applauds he looks terrified. He is there, you know, sort of cheering me up … last night he was there and I got stuck to the wall. Slowly, very slowly, like there was no gravity or something. *Mind the hole* he seems to whisper. With my hands I'm there, on the edges, but I would tear it up. I just can't, I fall.'

'You're pale man, and sweaty. Busy tomorrow morning?' Marc asks.

'Hopefully sleeping. These days I don't have any business.' I'm tired, words drip slowly, thoughts refuse to.

'Let's go to Oostende then. I'll drive, you can take a nap. Bring some water as well.'

Your orders, doc.

☼

Roaming through the city – longer days and nights up north.

What is this hammering inside? I know it, ought to spell it out. This is when I met those people, that girl Annie. The vomit I have to stand.

I don't blame this for happening, for changing me. I'm still here after all, roaming through the city: Place Royale and downwards, a straight line towards Grote Markt. I might be wrong but I imagine religious struggles being fought around here, foolish Anabaptists hung from municipal towers. *Fantasmagorie Baroque*. No, I'm surely mistaken; there are too few churches here for such struggles to have occurred. It had to be a hundred miles away – Antwerp, Münster et cetera.

Anyway. This hammering inside. I can't hide it: disclosure I long for.

Last time with Marc, at the coast, things started unravelling. I mentioned Annie, the two months I hung out with her friends – foolish people; money and drugs made them so. And Marc seemed more and more interested. He had a look that said 'I'm familiar with this'. I haven't seen him for a while now; I'm suspicious. He hasn't unveiled himself like I invited him to. I liked this 'you listen I talk' thing; now I'm under his spell.

But there are things he doesn't know yet. My own foolishness which brought me to this point. I want him to reveal himself.

☼

'I'm gonna tell you, Marc, much more than my dreams; I'm gonna tell it straight. Once I met a British girl, Annie. Pale, skinny, brunette. We played a weird game together. *How far will you go?* you might call it. I was sure I was the one who could go furthest. But sex with her was like inhaling asbestos. Deeper, harsher, colder: blindfold me, I'll clean you out. Lick it, I'm bleeding.

I was possessed, Marc. By what, you ask? I'm still wondering. The more defenceless I was, the more I raised the stakes. The more frightened, the more hysterical I became. Of what, you ask? That white hole I'm trying to get into, maybe – I was on cocaine every day; that took the fear away. I thought I could beat anybody. But her, she was like 'now that you're here, fight me'.

I almost killed her once. She brought friends, they were hidden somewhere in the apartment. She had tied me to the radiator beneath the bedroom window, by my ankles. She was harshly sucking me, biting. My raging excitement was about to explode onto her.

Two friends of hers, seemingly a couple, come out of somewhere in the apartment, pretending not to notice me. She is gently jacking him off; he comes on me. I'm still over-excited, a swordfish. They untie me, I'm wrecked, staggering. He tries to fuck me from behind, wiggling out I punch him in the testicles. Trying to run away, naked, frightened, hard as a cock, I stumble and fall. Annie laughs, stoned, her nose bleeding; she takes a coin from a tray alongside her bed, as if she were deciding my fate. I'm in pain. She takes a razor and comes straight at me, points to my cock, symbol of life, wants me raped. She comes closer, dull. I wait for her, beat her in the womb, where it hurts the most: the razor falls, she curls up in pain, crawling onto it with her breast. She bleeds, screams, laughs. The two animals over there, all of a sudden they exist again and run after me: they want me dead. I run away, out of the window, naked. I've kept running ever since, Marc; do you understand? Fight me - she meant it; and she won. I almost killed her in exchange. Do you understand?'

'I do, Josep. Why would I listen to you otherwise?'

'Well, Marc: unless you are as twisted as I am, you can't understand. But I guess you can, I guess you are.'

'You guess wrong my friend; I wouldn't find myself tied to a window and fucked from behind. But I do know what you mean.'

☼

'You're in Brussels, Josep. Just accept it. I was born here: do you know how many people I've seen earning at twenty five more than workers with over twenty years' experience? It breeds that weird arrogance – maybe it stems from the promiscuity of politics, diplomacy. I know you might think that this happens all over the world nowadays, or even that it has always happened. But trust me, this phenomenon has become overwhelming here – and it's not only about expats. You know there's still some sort of upper class nobility here? With very high profile parties, premeditated match-making and all that *noblesse oblige* kind of stuff? Some people think it's all about heads chopped off a few centuries ago – too few here, apparently ...'

What it is this guy trying to tell me? Class conflict? That's long gone ...

'Listen to me, Josep, it might help you figure out what happened. I had friends here that got mad about this circus of social arrogance, mad enough to lay a sort of trap. They didn't actually expect it to go as far as it did, but underneath that was probably their goal ... Anyway, they started to grab the attention of the city's mythomaniac freaks – big wallets, nice hairdos, muscular bodies and CVs - you know, getting introduced in the coolest places, spreading rumours about hard-core parties, drugs, orgies ... It was actually all about challenging them: *are you really so crazy-cool to do such and such a thing? Anything? Or wouldn't you dare?* It was, I have to admit, at our own risk ...'

Staring at me like a priest looking for guilt ...

'Once we were at Bar Rouge – that was the one and only time I actually took part in this game. We were trying to get some cocaine - classic pulp setting: the toilets. Now we were on the verge of getting into a fight with a dealer. One of the guys we persuaded to come along, Martin-the-German-diplomat, well, he lost his usual *aplomb*. He was actually terrified by the situation I had somehow forced him into: locked in a water closet, a dealer yelling at us and banging on the door, trying to break it down. Whether or not the dealer had a gun, I never found out; but he seemed quite persuasive. I thought, though, this guy just wants to show us how mad he can get if someone pulls three grams of cocaine out of his pocket, as we had done. At the same time, my impression was that he didn't want to make a major scene in there. Whatever the truth was, I told Martin: 'We've got two options here. Either we get out and take him on - no ceremony, no time for reaction. After all we're high and you're a German bear ... Or we go out and try to convince this guy that we were kidding, it was only a stupid bet. We pay him for the trouble and the three grams we stole and sniffed voraciously. Martin hesitated.

The unconscious certainty that nobody, not even that dealer, would have made a scene in that easy-fuck easy-drugs club, emboldened me. I gave Martin a coin. 'Heads,' I told him, 'we beat his ass, tails we negotiate'. 'Ok,' Martin replied hesitantly. Tails.

So we went out. I tried to explain to the screaming guy that we would have paid him off for any inconvenience: easier done than thought. He accepted and ran out. 'That coin saved your ass, *hein*?' I mocked him: 'Imagine if we would have gone at him ... a pussy like you, he would have beaten the shit out of you ...'

See Josep, that was enough for me at this point – I opted out. But the other guys, well, they made a rite out of that coin episode. 'Flip the coin, it will choose for you.' The perfect game for arrogant freaks ...'

Annie's hands before I got out ... They put it in her hands, foolishness followed ...

'Anyway. Once the bad things started happening – overdoses, hospitalisation – the guys who initiated this game gradually gave it up. Too much even for them. Still I'm amazed, you see, by those guys agreeing to play such a game, the ones who suffered its consequences. Why would they do it, Josep? You should know after all ... How would you get to this point otherwise? What pushed you? I guess it was the same thrill of recognition ... This - what would you call it? - archaic sense of 'your own reputation'; like pop-stars in the magazines ... Win the world oh cosmic egotist ...'

'You seem so proud looking back, Marc. It's like your experiment worked out. But it harmed me, irremediably. It got under my skin ... the situation that I found myself in with Annie, and then... the incapacity to react ... Three months have passed, yet I can't figure out what prevents me from regaining myself, something just switched off ... Consciously or not I keep going back to that last month I was dating Annie, and impotence, nightmares ... I'd love to just get it out, you know - yell, get angry, lose it! But I'd rather cry. And then this game you invented ...'

'See, Josep, I do owe you an apology for what happened, if somehow I triggered it. And since we're here, I'm gonna come clean too. You shouldn't think that you got to this point because someone purposefully orchestrated it against you. Or because it just happened. You probably got there because ... That game was so exciting to you, irresistible. Think why you did it – you've already started. You've unveiled, to me, dreams and roots, your perspectives and nature. That's the breakpoint, see? That's entirely up to you.'

'Stop arguing Marc, let me go. I'm gonna go.'

☼

Keep walking Pep, go. Oh it's damn windy.

Keep going, find your way home. 'No, haven't got a lighter, sorry.' Get out of my way, I can barely see you, can't you see?

They got you, you little puppet. So what?! Am I the only one? Surely not the last one ...

Oh here it is, Chaussée de Wavre ... *Joder* - still a long way home ...

So it should be my choice, up to me, right? Fuck you Marc …
I'm not gonna put everything back together, because … I've never
been there, never so deeply there …

Like everything therein has always been wrong – what do I do
then? Throw out the bad seed, cut away the bad fruit? This is me …

To face it, nothing but face it – whatever it is ...

Oh stinking stairs, home! Get something warm, get stoned, get to
sleep.

II

Away from the hype. It was spring when I met Marc. By the
summer I had left Brussels – forever, I thought then.

My father – bless him – owns a house in a little seaside village
on the Costa Brava. I didn't even need much explanation; I met him
twice upon my return, he just understood. 'Simplicity will do the
trick,' he said.

Life's rawness over here has opened a gateway through my head.
I've spent quite some time with deep-sea fishermen: you keep
listening, you actually learn from waiting. A question of limits.

☼

I haven't heard from Marc since I left Brussels; his words,
though, have long echoed in my mind.

I've been questioning myself. The least I can do; and the best
thing.

The most energy-consuming exercise is listening to the
thousands of hidden spirits climbing from the legs through the ribs
and upwards. You might tend to dismiss them; unless you're really
forced to go that deep, you would always pick an easier solution.

That's not my case anymore. You would fight against those thousand voices with all your strength – there's plenty of dark blue down there, it's no fun. But what would you get instead? Instincts fighting each other ... civil war, political scientists call it.

And instead. I myself have wanted to play the game that led me astray; and yes, I've suffered as much harm from it as I would have wanted to cause.

I haven't loved and have fed only my own passion – cosmic egotism, as Marc once put it. But that same stubborn instinct that once lost me has also brought me back. That very same unquenchable will wanted me to go deep down there and back again, whatever the risks, the scorn.

See? It's all about fine-tuning: somehow, pain is no pain.

April's breeze is calling now, I might go for a swim.

Monica Westerén

From Brussels South to Ottignies
The Story of Lia

If by living your dream you risk seeing it shatter to pieces,
then better to remain frozen. For ignorance is bliss,
and so are dreams that live forever.

15:39

Lasse calls me on my way to work to wish me good luck for my interview. I am struggling to keep the mobile phone to my ear with one shoulder while buttoning up my red and grey uniform – colours of Christmas, at least according to dad's Nordic traditions. By adding some further hints of red to our costumes, and giving us elf caps instead of the orthodox squared hats we're wearing today, we could make the whole train rock to the tune of Jingle Bells in the middle of summer. I picture children gaping silently at us, trying in vain to get the attention of their overworked parents, while excited Japanese tourists fill the train with high-pitched *Arigato goshaimashtas*.

My brother's voice on the phone brings me back to the wide avenue leading up to Brussels South Station.

'Hey dream child, ready to face the Swedes?' Lasse calls me *dream child*, but not in the sense of being all those traits and

53

characteristics any parent might wish for. It's more like a mockery of my tendency to drift off many times a day, to places far away.

'Hello Lars, I'm fine, how are you,' I tell my brother in a call centre voice.

'So, how are you gonna impress them? Pinker's *Language Instinct*, or something from Hassan? By the way, some of those prank calls by Lindström are just *hilarious* –'

'Lasse, I can't really talk now,' I interrupt my brother.

'Why, you're busy thanking God for his greatest gift to mankind?' I can sense Lasse's big brother smile at the other end of the line.

'Oh come off it, Lasse. I'm not Wallace, remember?'

'No, he's lousy – unlike you, a *real* star. Lia, the lovely … the lividly lovely linguist –'

'Oh just shut up, Lasse!' I interrupt my brother's chuckling. Usually I play along with his random word games, but today I'm tired. There is a short silence; I hear my brother taking a deep breath.

'What's wrong, Lia?' he asks and I hear his baby starting to cry in the background. I consider hanging up and blaming network problems next time we speak.

'Nothing, just late for the train.' I start walking faster, overtaking an elderly lady with a shopping cart made of kilt-like fabric.

'The train?' Lasse asks and I move the phone twenty centimetres away from my ear to prepare for the rest. 'The train?' he repeats, louder. My niece starts crying with greater intensity.

'Shhh Emma,' Lasse whispers, and she quiets down for a moment.

'Yes, the train – I need to *work*, just like you, like Mom, like Dad, like Maggie, even.' I'm breathing fast, faster than I'm walking.

'But Lia, the interview … what time –' I can see my brother gazing out of his window at the Montgomery roundabout, frustration written across his face, unwashed baby bottles and soft toys scattered around his feet.

'You know, Lasse, maybe dad has a point …' I start, suddenly feeling cold, despite the sunshine. 'I mean, I *do* want a family one day … And maybe Lund isn't the best place? Lindström isn't even lecturing there next year, apparently. I should have done more research …' I am shivering and my brother, for once, is speechless. I think of dad's words last night: languages are fun, but will they pay the bills?

'Lia, you're not serious,' Lasse tells me. 'Don't you see through dad? He's shit scared you'll make it, while he played it safe … Dad's getting old, you know –' I feel the anger boiling up again.

'He's an old chicken –' I blurt out. But then I feel guilty so I don't finish the sentence.

'OK, he's a chicken but you are *not*. You are going to go sit through your interview today and you're going to shine like a star and get that scholarship. OK?' Lasse is lecturing, again; transformed into his lawyer-self. And I'm not a good client. I feel like switching the roles around by asking him 'What about you, Mr Perfect, where did your dreams go? Lost them under a mountain of smelly nappies?' But instead I take a deep breath and slow down my speed-walking in order to prevent myself from hyperventilating.

'I won't make it, Lasse.' A car drives through a puddle next to me, splashing grey water on my grey uniform.

'Of course you will!' my brother exclaims, like he really means it. I laugh, feeling like I'm three years old again, having asked my mother if I would ever sit on the big toilet seat alone.

'It's at five, right, so you still have over an hour?' my brother pleads.

'I have to go Lars,' I tell him and wipe the dirty water off my face. I speed up significantly as I enter the crowded and badly signposted concourse of Brussels Midi, hoping that my Nordic walking pace will discourage lost travellers from approaching me. It's always risky to walk through a station in uniform.

'Tell me you're gonna go for it, Lia. Make Chomsky proud!'

'Sorry, gotta get on the train. I'll call you later.' I stop for a second in front of the departure screens, before continuing towards platform thirteen.

'Lia, this is your chance. You need to get *off* that train!'

'I'll get off when we've arrived.'

15:48

Ines greets me with a smile on the platform. They say in Swedish that *those with little wit laugh easily*, and this is definitely true in my colleague's case. She is so carelessly happy, painfully unaffected by the thought of yet another slow train ride.

'Salut, Lia. Klaar?' Ines rarely speaks more than five words in a row – she is as generous with language as the SNCB is with staff reductions. Nevertheless, she manages to mix and bastardise languages she does not even speak. I correct her in vain – she insists on apologising to German passengers about the *verspätnis* and not the *verzögerung*. Once she told a middle-aged American couple that in France the trains have *slut* machines. She's not a bad colleague, but her ignorance can make me want to stuff the whistle down her throat until nothing but frail bird-like sounds escape. Words should be kept for more noble mouths and more appreciative audiences than a simple Flemish ticket inspector on a delayed local train.

I need to use the toilet before we leave, so I reverse into one of the train's foul-smelling cabins and lock the door behind me.

'Hello ghost inspector,' I greet my white face in the mirror. Then I rummage through my inspector's bag to find my sun powder and rouge, maybe some lipstick. I take out the heavy ticket machine, my wallet, some change that has slipped out, keys, sunglasses, painkillers and tissues. There is no makeup. I look at the army of essentials on the window sill and sit down on the closed toilet seat. *No sun powder on the first and whitest day of summer – just my luck.* I shut my eyes and think of nothing for ten seconds. Actually, I try to think of nothing, but instead I think of Chomsky's transformational grammar because whenever I try to think of nothing I think of everything else. Then I think of sleeping and how nice it is to dream with your eyes open.

Sleep and dreams are my escape; an off-piste route at work. *Dormire, sova, dormir, to sleep, slapen, nukkua* – in which language will the passengers sleep today? When work is about travelling from A to B, day after day, the same scenery chugging by, you need a cave to retreat to. Sleeping is not quite a remedy, but dreams are a strong palliative for the aches and pains of adjusting to a life that isn't yours. When I sleep, I dream, and when I dream I am alive.

Watching other people sleep makes me feel less alone; it somehow calms my thoughts. Yesterday a young blond man spoke to me in his sleep throughout the journey. It was unusually quiet, with few people getting on between Ottignies and Brussels South, so I spent most of the evening watching people breathing and dreaming. The man's hair was as fair as I remember mine being, on sailing boats with grandparents in the Adriatic Sea. His body exuded safety; it slowed down the race of words, phonemes and morphemes running through my brain. When he spoke – his eyes open but with a distant and dreamy look – the constant flow of language components froze in action, like raindrops moving through a cold air front and turning into ice before hitting the ground.

'Where are you? Where did you go?' It wasn't the voice of a nervous child who is looking for his mother when waking up in the middle of the night. Nor was it the voice of a tired husband who is losing his wife to an over-demanding boss. It was a loving voice; a naïve voice looking to guide home hopeless cases and lost dreamers.

'I'm still here,' I replied. 'On the train.'

Three loud knocks on the door wake me up.

'Lia, are you there?' Ines' voice sounds worried. I open my eyes and feel my heart thumping. Another four knocks, more desperate now.

'We're off, Lia!' I look at my watch, which says 15:52. I get up from the toilet bowl, feeling slightly groggy, and start shovelling my essentials back into my inspector's bag.

'Are you ok, Lia?' Lia, Lia, Lia! Why does she repeat my name? I realise I have not yet responded to Ines' knocking, my own vigourous heartbeat submerged within its intrusive pulse.

'Yes,' I tell her, and open the door.

'Let's go, Lia! Inspection time!' She shakes my shoulders, like I am a sachet of sugar about to be poured into a coffee.

'Ready?' she asks. I feel for the heavy ticket machine in my inspector's bag, nod, and leave the small toilet without looking back.

15:54

The train is filling up, with two more minutes until departure. I wonder who I will meet today; what new accents and words I will encounter. I look forward to pleasant lisp-free Spanish from South America, and fast-spoken Czech – like a leaking tap that never stops dripping. When I meet Italians, I greet them in their language. The odd Finns you bump into in Belgium run the risk of being asked about the roots of their language – even when their faces and body language cry out in desperation for me to shut up. But I continue talking, listening and putting words together. It's like collecting grains of sand for a castle I know I will one day build. I know I will be able to use all the words, sounds and meanings my passengers hand out so freely, as if they were worthless.

'Toilets checked,' Ines tells me proudly while saluting me soldier-style, her right hand bouncing stiffly off her forehead.

'Great,' I tell her and wonder how she manages to be so into it all – toilets included.

'I found these. Yours?' She hands me three leaflets from Lund University. *Language is what differentiates human beings most from animals.* My dad's voice reappears for a moment; it's him reading the flyer to me, some years ago: *Language constitutes the most important precondition for the greater part of human activity, both social as well as technological.* Today I no longer hear dad; his language is dead. He's an old sick dog who doesn't bark, doesn't jump, doesn't eat anymore. I close my eyes and think about shaking hands with the Swedish delegation from Lund's Department of Linguistics. Then the train jerks and I feel dizzy; that's Ines blowing her whistle on the platform. No time to think about my PhD-to-be. We're pulling away from Brussels South, and there are tickets to check, passengers to control.

15:58

The air on the train is musty; it smells like a non-aired-out bedroom. I try to open the sliding windows but they are jammed. Passengers are fanning themselves with magazines, tickets and even receipts. The ones with bare legs sit at the edge of the seats in order to avoid getting their skin stuck to the blue plastic. They stiffen as they see me – some come running to explain that they need to buy a ticket because 'they were late'. Excuses. In how many different languages and shapes have they been delivered to me? Dutch, French, Italian, German, Spanish, Swedish …

'Allez Lia, stop dreaming and start *checking* people.' Ines – my watchdog. I try to go back to my language count but Ines ushers me further into the carriage where I am greeted by a bunch of sweaty students and a crying child. I dislike the Sunday afternoon trains with all the students returning to university. There is too much noise in too small a space; too many conversations in one setting. My temples are pounding.

16:00

My first passenger is a man with a wild beard and intense eyes, my dad's age. Despite the summer heat, he is wearing a neon green winter hat and is flipping something over and over again in his hand – it looks like a coin. There is something Scandinavian and vaguely familiar about his sunken face and white hair escaping from underneath the hat. I wish I didn't have to approach him, because I am sure he hasn't had a shower for months, but it's my job. Checking, selling and smiling – that's what I do.

'When do we get there?' he asks in a hoarse voice, like an impatient child on a road trip.

'Excuse me?' I can't believe he expects me to know his destination.

'When do we *arrive?*' he clarifies – only this, of course, does not clarify anything. I decide to go for the standard SNCB reply, void of any emotions.

'At 17:01 in Ottignies, sir.' I hate myself for sounding so factual; so much like a ticket inspector.

'What time is it now?' he asks, scratching his right ear. I look at my wristwatch and tell him it is four o'clock.

'Ah, time for a break,' he exclaims and digs out a Twix from his pocket. With long nails and dirty hands he offers me half of the chocolate bar.

'Or do you prefer Mars?' he sighs and throws a wide smile in my direction. Strange for a tramp to have such perfectly straight and white teeth.

'Man has to know his preferences,' he chuckles. I feel his eyes on me even after I have handed him his single ticket to Etterbeek.

16:04

'Prochain arrêt, Bruxelles-Central,' Ed announces at the front of the train. 'Cinq minutes de retard.' I'm one car behind schedule; I'll never make it through all the carriages before Ottignies.

I step out of the train after rearranging my red and grey hat, and wave to Ines at the other end of the platform. She waits for the last passengers to get on, a teenage boy helping his girlfriend step into first class. I smile silently to myself – they will be my *catch of the day*.

The carriage is empty apart from the teenage couple, their fresh youth clashing horribly with the seventies looking beige-with-a-hint-of-green seats. They are already absorbed in their books; her head on his shoulder, his hand on her thigh. OK, little lovebirds, let's see your tickets. Suddenly the boy speaks, softly.

'Kiscica,' he whispers and caresses her hair. I freeze. *Kiscica*. Little cat! That's what Gábor used to call Evelyn.

There is an aura of contentment and satisfaction surrounding them. *Little cat.* I want to be invisible and just observe their linguistic exchange of affection – adoration turned into words. Different languages have such different expressions of love – some do different variations of 'sweet', 'loved' or 'precious one'. *Rakkaani, älskling, mon chéri, tesoro*. Others do animals, parts of them or diminutives. *Bambolina, coniglietta, sötnos* – sweet nose of an animal. The boy hands me a paid-in-full ticket for two adults in first class; the girl continues reading. His beautiful hand – slightly tanned and very masculine – falls back to the girl's thigh after I hand him their stamped tickets. I feel at once empty and enriched while moving away from the couple, back towards second class.

16:09

The man in the green winter hat is waiting to use the toilet between the two carriages. He is still flipping a coin incessantly. There is a strong smell of urine and I am not sure where to look for the culprit – the homeless man in front of me, or Ines, who forgot to disinfect the toilet.

'You are late,' he tells me and points towards his wristwatch, as if it were my personal responsibility to get the train to its destination on time.

16:11

The next passengers I meet are young and winter-pale male students, discussing some professor called Jouglain.

'She is a bomb,' one of them with a large whitehead on his chin states.

'Oh come on, she's only just *drinkable*,' says a scrawny one with three hairs on his upper lip – a pathetic attempt at a moustache.

'I think she's a *cow*,' complains a third one with Prince Charles-like ears.

'You're just bitter because she gave you a D in macroeconomics,' Whitehead tells him, after picking something from his nose and flicking it across the aisle.

'That has nothing *to see with it*,' Prince-Charles-Ears counters. 'I just don't think she's anything special.' I note that 'it has nothing to see with it' is indeed correct in French, but would be 'nothing to do with it' in Swedish and 'does not enter into it' in Italian.

Then I turn into the Big Bad Wolf for a second and imagine the adolescents as Disney's Three Little Pigs, and think about scattering their course notes in Economics across the train carriage in one big blow. It makes me smile. Perhaps the best aspect of my job is reading the passengers and doing with them what I see most fit. I might adopt a small girl after I stamp her ticket, and challenge her to avoid licking her lips until the last bite of her sugar donut. I transform into a judge at a criminal trial and get to decide the fate of the middle-aged lady complaining about delays and increases in ticket fares. 'You get there faster when you're having fun,' as the SNCB states on its new website.

I never quite get there fast enough. My imagination runs dry before we reach the terminus, after which an empty return ride awaits me like the cold embrace of a wife who knows she is being cheated on. On days when there is a shortage of men travelling alone – the ones most likely to engage in a discussion with a ticket inspector – I can't wait to get to bed where dreams effortlessly appear.

16:16

The third carriage serves me two spoilt girls from Antwerp who are comparing notes on how terrible their lives are.

'I have no friends,' the one with a leather backpack says.

'I miss my family,' Leather Backpack's friend says and makes a sour face.

'My job sucks,' Leather Backpack says and sighs.

'Oooh,' Sour Friend says, compressing one of her fists with the other hand, until her knuckles crack. 'The pet shop is not so bad,' she continues in an 'ahhing' way.

'It could be worse, at least you're not a ticket inspector,' one of them whispers and then they both giggle. Little cunts. I swallow their criticism of my career choice with a forced smile and flatly wish them a *goede reis*, blaming it all on my father's incomplete linguistic mission, which landed him at the SNCB. I am still travelling down the very track he chose for me by getting me a summer job as a train signaller at Brussels Zuid in the summer of 1999.

It could be worse, indeed. I could be working on the bullet trains in Japan, where talking to the ticket inspector is as acceptable as sneezing in public.

I am struck by an unpleasantly familiar smell, and I know that he is back. *Is he following me?* I move faster through the carriage, to prevent the homeless man from catching up with me, but have to stop to sell a ticket to a man in a beige raincoat and brown bowler hat. The middle-aged passenger reminds me of someone who once flashed me in a dark park in Oxford, and I wonder if this one is wearing anything underneath.

'How safe is your train?' The slurring voice behind me comes from someone who nurses hangovers with whiskey rather than Nurofen. I turn around and see the man with the neon green winter hat pointing at me with a small red object. It looks like one of our emergency hammers.

'Give me that, Sir!' I snap at the tramp, as my safety inspector instinct kicks in. 'Where did you find it?'

'Over there,' he nods and points backwards with his thumb, like a bus driver telling the passengers to move away from the front entrance. I try to snatch the red hammer from him but he hides his hand behind his back. Then he leans over, swaying from one side to the other while enveloping me in his old alcohol breath.

'Watch out,' his whiskey basso states. 'Or there's going to be an accident.'

'Give me that,' I repeat and point towards the red hammer. The man lifts his gaze, tries hard to focus on me and points at my chest with his free index finger.

'In case of emergency,' he mumbles. 'It could be your only way out … Smash! Right through there –' The man barks and slices through the air with his red hammer, in the direction of one of the train's double-glazed windows. The rapid movement nearly makes him lose his balance. He grabs my shoulder to stop himself from falling; I take a step back and nearly trip. The reeking man's upper body comes close to collapsing on me and I panic. In a single action I push him to the side and escape to the next carriage.

16:21

I must confiscate the red hammer. But I have more tickets to sell and stamp, so I decide to wait until I can ask Ines. She knows the procedures. Besides, I know she'd very much enjoy claiming back property of the SNCB; waving her self-righteous index finger at misbehaving passengers. So instead of going back to the tramp, I move on to my fourth carriage, where a Flemish-British pensioner couple are complaining about the lack of catering facilities on Belgian trains. Their trivial conversation calms me down.

'A little restaurant carriage would be super,' exclaims the woman with boots, gloves and handbag in matching golden retriever skin – she obviously does not believe in summer wear.

'Or a friendly lady pushing a coffee cart through the carriages,' her bald husband answers in a slightly overexcited voice. 'I could use one now!' he exclaims with a lazy tongue. I wonder if he's referring to the friendly lady, the coffee, or both.

'Yes, I'm quite thirsty, actually. Appelsap would be *fantastisch*!' the blue-eyed wife pants. I note that we *have* thirst in Flemish, but *are* thirsty in English and Swedish.

'Allez Lia. You're *drifting*.' Why can't Ines mind her own business? She should be at the other end of the train!

'Stop analysing the poor pensioners' choice of words,' she winks at me. I hate her simplicity, her straight-forwardness and her voluminous hair. Next to her lion's mane, I am like a wet cat on heat, leaving behind a trail of fine blond hair. I decide against giving her the pleasure of reclaiming SNCB property.

'Get lost Ines,' I hiss, and try to go back to the thought she interrupted: whether languages in general differentiate between human and animal hair. But I know my linguistic analysis is redundant on this train; there is no space for the endless flow of words, running circles in my mind like an assiduous hamster. I am tired of my own fixation with languages; I want my brain to shut down. Always linking and interpreting, always analysing words and sentences. My curse is having grown up in Brussels with a Finno-Swedish father and an Italian mother. Why wasn't I born in a homogenous society, like Iceland?

As we head north, just to be able to leave the city from the south end, I contemplate leaving the analysis of phonemes and morphemes to the experts. While adjusting my red and grey inspector's hat, I decide that Brussels Schuman will make a good graveyard. It is time to bury my language obsession once and for all. Anyway, there is barely half an hour left and I would never make it for the interview.

16:26

There is no time for mourning, because the world is full of free riders. Next up, I can't resist asking Swedes for their tickets in their mother tongue. I love to see their surprised look as they realise an outsider has just stepped into their closed-off sphere of intimacy. I want to analyse their accents and choice of words; I want to guess which region they are from. I want to talk about idioms and their link to the Nordic mentality like *there is no bad weather, only bad clothes,* and *let the food silence the mouth.* But instead we engage in small talk, bereft of interesting words.

'Where are you from?' Their accent tells me they are from somewhere in central Sweden.

'How long have you lived in Brussels?' Maybe Värmland? There is something twisted about the 'l' in their *Bryssel*.

'What are you studying? Enjoying your summer job here?' Their ignorance slices me in half – I just nod, instead of clarifying that my job is permanent. I realise they are from Örebro – same rhythm as my cousins when they speak. Naïve Swedes who have grown up in a safe bubble stretching only as far as the neighbouring town of Kumla. Happily unaware Swedes who don't see that opportunities are not there for everyone. I pity them and their childhood of biking in reflective vests in car-free zones; their teenage years of secret beer drinking in their parents' summer cottages; their easy rides through school without numbered grades. If this is the wisdom that awaits you after state-subsidised day care, cumulative child allowance, and general Master's Degrees in Social Science, then no part of me wants to trade places with them. Not a single bone. I say *hejdå* to them but they have already turned back to their game of travel chess.

An olive-skinned woman across the aisle from the Swedes is squirming in her seat and I know she has not bought a ticket. I think of all the excuses she will make: 'The ticket machine was broken'; 'I don't understand the language'; 'the train is always late' … I'm so tired of free riders.

'Ce l'ho,' the free rider says in a mouse-like voice. Her hand searches through the bag in a frenzy. No, no, elegant lady, you will not get away this time. Then she pulls out a printed piece of paper, unfolds it and hands it over.

'Ah voilà Madame, le ticket!' she says with a heavy Italian accent and sits back down with a relieved sigh. Impossible.

'Non è valido, signorina,' I say and look her straight in the eyes. The colours are exquisitely blended, just like her whole complexion and outfit. As if she had analysed her eyes and chosen her character and style accordingly.

'Ma perché?' she asks in a sincerely worried voice and puts down a thick book on the seat next to her. *Linguistica cognitiva*. I break into a sweat and my heart starts pounding faster. I know this book – I got it last Christmas from Lasse and Maggie. I know this wonderful book that attempts to explain the miracle of life through a clash of languages, not of culture. Suddenly the Italian lady transforms in my eyes. The afternoon sun seeps in through a narrow window that someone managed to slide open; it lights up her head from behind. I want to touch her long dark hair and make four-plated braids like my mother and I used to when I was a child. Her hair is just like mum's – the length, the texture is the same, only shinier.

'*Lentokonesuihkuturbiinimoottoriapumekaanikkoaliupseerioppilas*,' I tell her slowly, tasting every syllable of the beautiful word.

'I'm sorry?' She pretends not to be interested.

'Technical warrant officer trainee specialised in aircraft jet engines – world's longest word; it's actually used by the Finnish Air Force!' Counting the thirty six syllables makes me feel warm inside.

'Finnish? Sorry, I don't speak Finnish.'

'Yeah, Finnish. They also have the world's longest palindrome.'

'Palindrome?'

Bella Italia; she's starting to annoy me. Doesn't she know anything about languages?

'A word or phrase that reads the same backwards as forwards, like *saippuakauppias* – soap salesman. Or *saippuakalasalakauppias* – black market soap fish salesman, but I don't know if you'd ever actually say that.' No, *she* wouldn't, I'm starting to realise. Her slow reactions disappoint me, make me angry. What kind of linguist is not into palindromes or syllable-racing? I present her with my favourite Finnish dialogue, as a last resort:

'You know, Finns love their summer … And what they do is, they make a big fire. To celebrate that it's so bright. It's beautiful!

I've done it myself –' I pause for a second to give the Italian lady space to react, but she says nothing.

'Imagine you were out in the Finnish archipelago, and I told you *kokoo kokoon koko kokko*, what would you tell me?'

'Scusa?' My passenger asks, so I continue explaining.

'Well, you would ask *koko kokkoko*? And then what would I answer? *Koko kokko,* plain and simple. Isn't that hilarious? Like some tribal language – Kokoo kokoon koko kokko. Koko kokkoko? Koko kokko! Better than the click languages of Africa.'

My voice comes out too high-pitched, so I clear my throat. The Italian lady is squirming more in her seat now than before, when she couldn't find her ticket. I know I've reached a dead end, but I just have to tell her what it all means.

'It means *put together all the branches for the midsummer fire. The entire midsummer fire? Yes, the entire midsummer fire,* I mumble and look down to my black shoes. I notice one of them has a brown stain. When I look up, the Italian lady and her Cognitive Linguistics bible are still staring at me, motionlessly. How embarrassing – she gives me that blank stare you give to children who invent stories about invisible friends. I turn around to walk towards the next carriage, which I know is full of free riders and unchecked passengers, when I hear the Swedes again. The Swedes with their safe suburban smiles; smiles that speak of dental gargling at primary school for seven minutes every day.

'As I said, we all make choices.'

'Of course, on a daily basis. Some choose to travel the world while young ...'

'Others choose to stay in the safety of their hometown ...'

'And some people keep travelling, but always to the same places...'

My stomach makes a washing machine movement and I know I have to get away. How dare they talk about me, in Swedish, when they *know* I understand? My vision is blurry, but it looks like the 'WC' sign is unlit at the far side of the carriage. Then I see him again, the man with the wild beard. He is still flipping his coin but without paying any attention to it. Like my aunt knitting while watching TV, except there is no TV, just me. The red emergency hammer is nowhere to be seen. His blue watery eyes scan me from top to bottom, in a factual X-ray manner, not the way a man normally checks out a girl. *It's OK, stop being silly. Just a homeless person entertaining himself; he won't harm me.* I feel his eyes on me as I pass his row. Then, suddenly, he grabs my inspector's bag. I turn towards him and see him smiling his supra-white smile, but he is not holding on to the bag. It has caught on the handle of a suitcase left in the aisle next to him.

'You are stuck,' he tells me. Or asks me? It's hard to tell from his slurring voice. I unbuckle my bag and rush towards the door.

'Pay attention to your passengers!' he calls after me. I cross Ines on my way to the toilet and tell her 'Be careful, he's a freak'. Who, she asks, and I point behind me towards the homeless man.

'We should throw him off, he's harassing me,' I tell Ines, while hugging my inspector's bag as if it was a teddy bear.

'Who?' Ines repeats and I point to the seat which had been taken up by the homeless man – but is now empty. She raises an eyebrow and asks if I'm OK.

'Not really,' I tell her and lock myself in the toilet.

16:38

I see a hollow face in the mirror, it's like I am transparent and blending into the beige walls of the toilet cubicle. I press the pedal below the sink to wash my face, but there is no water. Ines forgot to ask for a refill. Something is glimmering next to the small metallic washbasin. *You are stuck, pay attention* – the man's words are still ringing in my ears. This is a farce; am I going crazy? I slap myself in the face, once, twice, three times. I lean over the washbasin to catch my breath. Then I see the coin. *His* coin? I panic and look around. I expect to see him entering through the slot of the paper towel dispenser, through the window, through the keyhole. Someone knocks on the door. I close my eyes and press my palms over my ears. The knocking turns into banging – 'get out, get out, get off'. I breathe out – it's not the tramp. But that voice, I know it. What's *he* doing on the train? I can't face him; I can't take his nagging voice, his excitement over words, like Gogol's *Akakij Akakijevitj*. It's only words, dad, words! Why are you following me? This is my life, dad!

Suddenly it hits me and I am thrown forward by the impact. My life. I'm about to repeat history. As the train makes an abrupt stop, I look at my wristwatch, which tells me it's 16:43. I take the coin and throw it in the toilet bowl; it makes a clanging sound when it hits the metal at the bottom. Then I use my right foot to activate the flush, and the coin disappears down the tracks together with a flow of bright blue liquid. We have arrived at Etterbeek – *a perfect place for resurrection.*

'I'm getting off,' I tell Ines when stepping onto the platform.

'Of course you are honey, that's our *job*.' There is something sweet about her ignorance.

'No, I mean getting *off* off. Like *leaving* this train business.' I hand over my inspector's bag and my hat to Ines as a symbolic gesture, in case she still doesn't get it. Then I simply walk off. *This one's on me, you lucky bastards* – it's a happy day for free riders.

16:48

There is still time – all I have to do is get to the ULB. I turn left along Boulevard General Jacques towards the university. There is traffic-related chaos at the junction where it meets Avenue de la Couronne; it looks like the traffic lights are not working and there's been an accident. A man and a woman are facing each other, shouting, pointing fingers at each other's cars. An ambulance whizzes by, piercing my ears. Two policemen are directing traffic and one of them tells me to stop at the pedestrian crossing.

'There's been an accident,' the policeman says. 'A *rail* accident,' he specifies.

The words in my head stop, and the cars take over. I watch them drive round and round in circles, militantly following the policemen's orders. I think of Lund University, the course in cognitive linguistics, I think of dad, I think of Lasse. I think of the tramp with the red hammer; small but deadly. I know I need to move now, in order to make my interview. But I feel dizzy; cannot walk. The world is spinning, hands waving, policemen dancing, cars hooting, racing around me, across me and over me. Dogs barking, sirens tearing up my eardrums.

And then silence.

I open my eyes and take the mobile phone out of my uniform pocket to call dad. He doesn't answer, phone is dead, cannot be reached at the moment. I leave a message; I leave two messages and another missed call before I start walking again. It feels good to be outside in the sun, without my hat.

17:00

Somewhere in the capital of Europe, the city of dream careers and lost paths, a train headed for Ottignies has stopped in its tracks. Its destination is one minute away on paper; yet it will be hours before the train arrives. The ticket inspector has gone missing. An accident? Engine failure? Why the loud noise? Did someone really jump out? How? Passengers' questions remain unanswered. Some metres away, a homeless man is lying on his back with cuts across his face; his drying blood sinking into the fresh earth. The million tentacles of wet grass embrace him and his small red escape tool. His hair as light as a Scandinavian summer night; long dancing wisps in the world's Eastern windy city. Shattered pieces of glass glistening like jewellery around his neck. His beard reaches down to his chest, where his closed fists are resting, knuckles facing the sky. He is smiling the smile of a noble man, with white and straight teeth from a toothpaste ad. He is counting the clouds, following their race towards darkness. He sighs and then he closes his eyes. His hands relax, opening up like two white lilies, one of them revealing a silver coin that glimmers in the afternoon sun.

Nick Jacobs

The Commissioner and the Pig

The story of Richard

07:15

I'm lying on my side as everything comes into focus. Roger Moore has his gun cocked and is staring straight into my eyeline from the *Moonraker* poster above my desk. I've been told I look good in a tux. Firing a gun looks easy enough. Maybe it's finally time to start plotting my own route to the 007 role? I'll email that friend at the New York film school today. Of course there are other details to be arranged - sabbatical leave, sub-letting the flat, plane ticket. Is it still off-season?

The alarm goes off for a second time, and the idiocy of the thought process descends. I throw off the covers and bounce lopsidedly to my feet. A sheet of lined paper has blown off the desk during the night and sticks to the sweaty underside of my foot. I brush it off and head straight for the mirror. Disappointment, in its daily dose.

As I visualise the day in front of me, I realise there is little I can do to get ahead. All I can hope is that the Commissioner is in a better mood than yesterday. I can still hear her words after the error I made at the press conference: 'That made us all look silly'.

The note on the kitchen counter draws my attention just as I am dipping a spoon into my corn flakes.

Away until Friday. Use the open soy milk in the fridge. M

Is that an order or an invitation? Too late either way. The kitchen, like our flat-share, feels smaller than it should. The counters are off-white, thanks to a purple-coloured residue that looks like blackcurrant yoghurt. I run my hand along the sticky surface and move across to the open window for a gasp of fresh air. A warm sensation around my crotch tells me that the radiator directly below the window is piping hot and must have been on all night.

'For fuck's sake,' I call out of the window. A bird caws back a cry of desperation.

I urinate with my eyes closed, but cannot break into a fully liberating flow. I pull the flush with my free hand at what I estimate is about five seconds before the urination will end. The rush of water is gone in a flash, and a dribble of urine continues down into the pan, staining the water yellow. I exit the bathroom and the flat.

11:00

The Commissioners are in their weekly meeting and the office is quieter than usual. Spokespeople, assistants and low-level bureaucrats walk the corridors at a slower pace, lingering over the printer and at each other's desks. Mine looks in need of a tidy. I thought I had perfected the filing system but new objects keep cropping up and resisting categorisation. Personal travel bookings, emergency deodorant. The unattributed clutter has spread across the entire surface.

'Cup of tea, anyone?' Dirk calls from across the room. His English is impeccable.

'No thanks mate,' I reply with a smile. It's my first of the day and it feels creaky.

Over by the window, Eleni finally tears herself away from an article that has been making her laugh. 'You're making tea, darling? I don't want one now, thank you.'

Dirk, Eleni, the Commissioner and I: our team. A fifty-year-old career politician, personally and politically liberal like her native Holland. Dirk, her countryman and press assistant, elegantly greying in his mid-forties, a keen hunter of deer in the Ardennes. And Eleni. A name that resonates through these corridors. A twenty-six-year-old Greek intern with thick, wavy reams of jet-black hair, olive green eyes and summery dresses that grip her body like a greedy hand. Everyone desires her – it's only the degree of self-denial that changes.

Then there's me. Richard Cohen, thirty two, spokesperson to the Commissioner. *Wow*, people say when I tell them what I do. My job has EU in the title and enough digits in the salary to silence any doubters. Little do they know that I spend my afternoons trading film memorabilia online and contemplating potential wanking material for the evening ahead. What do I look like? Suit, hair, face, the usual. The underwhelming product of endless futile hours staring into mirrors, rearranging my fringe, contorting my face into a thousand different expressions in the hope of striking gold. And failing each time, shrinking back into resignation, cheeks sucked in and hands gripping the sink.

This morning should be a sedate affair. The diary is empty and the phone has yet to start ringing. But I can't stop replaying the press conference in my head. The pedantic, bearded vole in glasses: 'Why is the EU continuing to trade with Iran despite the brutal crackdown on protesters?' The response. The lack of notes. The lack of euphemisms. The use of real words.

I scan my emails and try to shake the memory. I reply to a pending request from a Slovakian journalist. All of the data is on our website. Don't hesitate to call if you need more info. *Do* hesitate, I implore him, as I hit reply.

I glance furtively around the office, and open Microsoft Word. I'm looking for a file saved as *LP*. Love Poetry. The quiet in the corridor emboldens me to open it. The page is scattered with disparate phrases.

My heart is an empty page. Will you caress it with words or hold a flame to its dog-eared corners?

Pretty raw.

You are Europe. Your hair is a Scandinavian wilderness, your thigh is like a Greek olive tree.

In the cold light of morning the passage feels nauseating. I consider staring at Eleni for more immediate inspiration. She is wearing red today, probably her best colour. She catches me looking at her, and I pan my eyes gently across to the window. Forget her, I tell myself. This is *love* poetry. And she is desire. The kind of desire that unseats healthy thoughts and brings you back to square one. I hear Dirk's heavy footsteps in the corridor and quickly minimise *LP*. I look for something innocuous to take its place on the screen, and find a journalist's email query about banana tariffs.

On the way back from the toilets I spot Juan, a stubbly intern known as Johnny following an incident with a condom and a beer bottle.

'Hey Richard!' he shouts along the corridor. 'El Inglés! ¿Qué tal tío?'

'Bien, ¿y tú?'

'¡Bien!' he grins back. And without breaking stride he shakes my hand and walks on, leaving me in no-man's-land. When I return from the toilets Johnny is next to Eleni, crouched down and marauding, her eyes fixed on the computer screen and his flitting greedily between the PC and her flawless face. He hits the mouse and suddenly they both erupt into laughter.

'I can't believe Marek was that drunk!' Eleni shouts. They click again and more incredulous laughter rings out. Then they are cast into silence as the computer stalls. Their eyes are locked on the faltering screen with mouths agape, primed for laughter. Sure enough, a few seconds later the cackling erupts. I open a new Word file and type the word TWAT in capitals, font size 26, then delete it. An email pops up in the corner of my screen and I snatch at it.

Dirk Van Bonders: 'Does he really think he's gonna get more than a laugh from her?'

I issue a sharp burst of laughter and turn it quickly into a cough. Swivelling round to my right, I see the back of Dirk's chair and above it his bushy mop of multi-tone grey. Steam rises above his head as he blows gently into his tea.

My mobile rings and I flee impulsively into the corridor.

'Do you like sausages and dumplings?' says a familiar voice. 'Well I hope so. We're heading to Poland next month.'

The Commissioner has changed her tune – last thing yesterday she sounded ready to hand me over to the Iranian authorities to do whatever they saw fit with me.

'It's that forum on boosting Eastern European export industries. The President has decided we need to be more visible in the member states, especially during the downturn. So Warsaw's back on the agenda, I'm afraid.'

I note it down illegibly on my palm and curse at the loss of another weekend. Another conference, an airless hotel lobby buzzing with badge-wearing delegates, word after word pouring out of a big gaping arsehole with multiple faces. Sustainable benchmarks, streamlined efficiency targets, free USB sticks for all.

'Richard,' she intones, noting the brevity of my responses. 'Let's forget about yesterday. They shouldn't have sent you up there without notes. That's not your fault. But be extra careful on Iran for now. Better not to say anything sometimes.'

'Point taken,' I reply.

'You know what those journalists are like when they get a juicy story like that. Wolves!'

Her gentle Dutch accent turns the final 's' into a 'sh', softening her phrase.

'So I'll see you later for the thing with the farmers?' the Commissioner asks.

'Yep, sounds good, see you then.'

'Wait a second, Richard. Can you put me on to Helena?'

'You mean Eleni?'

'Whoever it was that provided me with those notes on services liberalisation.'

I recall Eleni fretting over the notes yesterday, and losing the first file at around six, to a chorus of frightening Greek swearwords. Johnny has finally departed, leaving her to click through the photos for a second time. I cross the office, but she fails to notice until I am standing right next to her. I cup my palm over the receiver and whisper: 'It's the Commissioner for you'. I watch her eyes miss a blink.

Five minutes later, she hands the phone back to me and storms out of the room, fanning her face with her hands in a mad frenzy. I think about going after her, but am ultimately too repulsed by the idea of hearing myself throw tender platitudes at her. Besides, it's nearly midday. The journalists are filing in with their smug faces and mischievous questions. I'll need all my best platitudes for that.

14:30

From where I'm standing at the Schuman roundabout, all I can see are columns of cars leaping out of the underpass. They all seem to be a variation on grey - silver, chrome, charcoal. It is drizzling lightly and the droplets are colder than they should be in June.

I wish they would hurry up with this damn photo-shoot. The Commissioner is getting tetchy. She is checking her shirt, her jacket, her earrings. Her smile is souring by the minute. I check through the emails on my Blackberry to ensure that this is definitely *not* my fault. There it is: *2.30, Schuman roundabout*. I was right. It must be Gerhardt from the Bavarian farmers union getting the times wrong again. I thought they were meant to be good with punctuality ... I stop myself from making the joke. There is probably a German among the camera crew.

'Richard,' the Commissioner calls across to me. 'Well handled at the midday.'

I nod back, and start to reply, but a chorus of dissonant tractor horns drowns out my words. The tractors emerge from the park, where the farmers have been camped out for some form of protest involving barbecues and live cow milking. The vehicles crawl towards us in a haphazard formation, enjoying the freedom of the roundabout afforded them by the police cordon. The Commissioner fluffs up her hair to ensure that it has not lost any volume in the drizzle. Then she smiles. The wide, anticipative one she reserves for these occasions. Her cheek muscles look ready to buckle, like a train put simultaneously into forward and reverse.

Gerhardt finally approaches, alongside a farmer and his prize pig. When they arrive, the pig looks bewildered. It digs its snout into the muddy grass of the roundabout, and then kicks its head back in panic as it finds itself surrounded by suited bureaucrats. The Commissioner goes straight across to the farmer brandishing a handshake.

'That's quite a beast you've got there,' she says, looking straight at the man and keeping his hand in her grip for a few seconds.

'Ja!' the farmer replies, and they laugh together. We all laugh. The laughter should cut through the awkwardness, but instead it seems to suspend it in the air.

'So let's take a photo with this beauty.' She pats the pig's neck and pulls back sharply as it squeals. They line up for the photo: the Commissioner, the farmer and the pig. Gerhardt is momentarily redundant. After failing to interest the journalists in his petition, he heads in my direction.

I pre-empt him with some small-talk: 'Hello, how are things? Busy at the moment I'd imagine?'

'You *can't* imagine …' he starts, and I switch off. *Busy*. Busy organising conferences to tell people what they already know, but in bullet points. Busy catching up with people we have never really known. Busy flushing toilets and deleting emails. Gerhardt is coming to the end of an anecdote about an outbreak of bluetongue disease in a herd of Bavarian cattle.

'So do you get back to Bavaria much?' I cut in. It is a perfect tangent, fully masking my failure to listen. A text message buzzes in my pocket. I halt Gerhardt for a minute, provoking an awkward chuckle. Message from: Eleni. The word still threatens to excavate my stomach in a second, its power undiminished by this morning's gratuitous tears.

The Slovakian journalist called, he wants you to ring bak by 3. E

The tone punctures my excitement. I imagine her sending it in careless haste, rushing to get back to photos of drunken interns and leering men. Gerhardt's anecdote rumbles on and frees me to plan out my evening. I am suddenly crestfallen as I remember that work will not end at six tonight, but nearer eleven, when our weary chauffeur-driven Mercedes creeps back into Brussels after a public forum in Northern France. *What the EU does for You*, or something to that effect. The combination of visualising the event and listening to Gerhardt is particularly unpleasant. The Commissioner is already being whisked off for her next engagement by the deputy head of cabinet, and I make my excuses before trudging back into the open metallic arms of the Berlaymont.

22:35

The motorway back to Brussels is quiet. Matthias the driver is expressionless, barring a moment of rage - *Godverdomme* - when a four-by-four cuts in front of us without indicating. He catches my eye in the rear-view mirror. A thought flashes across his face but he stifles it. Perhaps something about women drivers?

The Commissioner has taken her place alongside me on the back seat, as is customary for our mini debriefings. Her eyeliner is slightly smudged and she has pulled a purple, woollen jumper over her evening dress. It is as much a statement as anything else, a message to self that she is now unequivocally off-duty. The change is enough to take the edge off. And she is talking with more abandon than usual. This is her way of telling me I've done my job well tonight. I reciprocate with a non-committal smile.

'When that idiot on the front row asked me why he should care about the EU, I was genuinely lost for words!' she cries, and we both laugh. There is a sense of hysteria between us - some kind of release from the airless sterility of the Vouziers public forum.

'He was right,' she continues. 'If he spends his life in that depressing village, drinking cans of cider and watching repeats of Friends doubled into French, then he doesn't need to know anything about the EU!'

I am too tired to correct her English, or to question her stereotypes, which bother me more than my own. A few minutes later, she calls out something to Matthias in Dutch. He nods his head, and half a kilometre later, we pull into the motorway services. The Commissioner lights up a cigarette outside the entrance and I dash inside for a mini-pack of Pringles. She is still smoking when I re-emerge through the glass doors.

'Richard, come join me for a moment. Best to get some fresh air. We still have another hour of driving ahead.'

'The air's not so fresh when you're blowing smoke everywhere,' I say flatly.

She laughs and tells me to shut up. We stand side by side and contemplate the car park. A couple are having a heated argument in a parked Ford Fiesta while two little boys practise handstands on a dogshit-infested patch of grass in front of the vehicle. They cast nervous glances back through the windscreen.

'Marriage,' the Commissioner sighs, puffing out a mouthful of smoke and provoking a cough on my part. 'Better to keep your freedom, Richard, or you'll be ...' Her face clenches into a tight-lipped smile as she searches for the right expression. 'Onder de plak. Under the ...'

'Thumb,' I say. She doesn't mind me finishing her sentences if it means efficiency.

'And losing your freedom isn't the worst part,' she continues. 'It's forgetting what freedom feels like. After so long you hardly recognise what true feelings are when they arrive. Makes it harder to ... grab them by the balls!' she adds, laughing with acidic gusto. She has been overusing this expression since I taught it to her. I pray that she never blurts it out in a press conference.

Her confessional tone makes me uncomfortable, but it is hardly new. Recently she has been stepping up the attacks on her husband Willy. He *is* a sour old bastard, by all accounts. And she is certainly not one to go down quietly with the marital shipwreck.

'Let's get back on the road. We don't want to be too tired for tomorrow,' I say, surprising myself with the softness of my tone.

'Are you going to offer me one of your crisps first?'

'Wasn't planning on it.'

I hold the Pringles out in her direction. She takes a couple, inspects them for a moment, and then bites into them noisily.

As I open the rear door Matthias jerks upright and searches for the radio tuner. His cheeks burn as the Flemish love ballad plays on and reaches an echoey guitar solo. He finally locates the off-switch and the eighties synth drumbeat grinds to a halt.

'Klaar?' he calls stiffly into the back. Ready. One of the handful of Dutch words I've picked up on these journeys. 'Ja,' the Commissioner calls back.

As we approach the Brussels ring road, a thought strikes me.

'Bollocks,' I blurt out. She doesn't recognise the word and looks perplexed. 'We forgot to go over the notes for tomorrow morning.'

'You're right,' she replies, closing her eyes for a moment.

'The car lobby will be hammering you with questions about the Korean deal. Shall we get in an hour early to prepare?'

'No,' she says. 'We're both pretty awake now, let's get it over with. Your place isn't too far from here is it?'

I search for reasons why we should not use my flat but fail to find anything concrete, and I give Matthias instructions on where to exit the ring. We start to wind through the sleeping suburbs of Woluwe. Elegant *fin-de-siècle* houses stand side by side at grossly varying heights, like adolescent boys lining up for a photograph. Minutes later we turn into my road, a nondescript side street lined with young birch trees.

The Commissioner has her eyes glued to the window. I wonder why she did not suggest her own house. We have worked there before, and her big study feels like an extension of the office. Perhaps the situation with Willy is worse than I thought. An extra hour could be the difference between finding him awake or asleep. Matthias offers to wait outside my building or find a local bar, but by the look on his face he's thinking about the strip club we passed on exiting the ring. The Commissioner tells him to go home and get some rest. A taxi will see her home later.

'So, this is where you take refuge from work,' she says, as I hit the lights in the corridor and slide the paper recycling pile out of the way with my shoe. 'Well I'm sorry to invade it with directives and free trade agreements. I hope we don't disturb your flatmate, Miranda is it? The one who works at NATO?'

'She's away in the States,' I call back from the kitchen, where I'm sweeping errant corn flakes off the counter and into my hand. Her recall of detail surprises me.

She has made her way into the lounge and I find her perusing my DVD collection.

'Of course, you're a James Bond fan. So - I've got to ask you a question,' she says, turning back towards me. 'Who is the best Bond?'

'Roger Moore,' I reply. 'I think Sean Connery's overrated.' She looks avid for detail so I elaborate. 'Roger Moore's touch of humour makes Bond more human, and that's what we all love about him. For me Bond isn't a ruthless killer, he's just a charming Englishman abroad.'

'Like you?' she asks casually, still studying the row of DVDs. A smile creeps across her face. It's an unfamiliar one, and I have trouble pinning it down.

'So which one of the Roger Moore movies is the best?' she asks, running her fingers over a cast-iron model of Bond's Alfa Romeo GTV6 from *Octopussy*.

I start to expound the multiple virtues of *Moonraker* - cinematic and narrative – but I become disturbed by the intensity of her gaze. She is actually listening, and I start to doubt whether the fact that Roger Moore barely used a stunt double is appropriate subject matter for an EU Commissioner. I leave the eulogy unfinished.

'Make yourself comfortable, I'll be one minute,' I call as I head towards the toilet, remembering the yellow residue. I have no need to urinate, and kill a few seconds contemplating myself in the circular mirror. My face has a resilient energy to it, despite my wilting posture and sluggish limbs. A shade of black stubble is emerging, giving my unremarkable face just a touch of the enigmatic. I flush and exit the bathroom.

00:20

'Let's pretend that I'm French and I'm particularly concerned about job losses arising from a trade deal,' I premise, about half an hour into our preparation. 'What will you be doing to ensure zat ze jobs at ze Toulon Renault factory are not lost when ze cheaper Korean cars arrive on ze European market?' I ask.

'I am *deeply* concerned about job losses at European plants,' she says, choking down a laugh. 'But let's remember that EU funding tools exist for diversifying the workforce.' Her tone turns more serious. 'French automobile workers could soon be retraining as ... astronauts!' She emits a schoolgirl laugh.

'Come on, be serious.'

'How can I when you're doing that ridiculous accent? Oh I don't know, Richard, I'll say something about parallel job creation from Korean firms setting up new plants in Europe. But I guess you don't trust me to put it into good English?'

'Just don't invent any more proverbs.'

'Don't tempt me!'

After a few more minutes of half-hearted preparation, a thought dawns on me with unusual clarity. I do not want her to leave. The absurdity of it, the Commissioner here on my couch, draining cans of Jupiler at quite a pace, has become the most natural thing in the world. And somehow less absurd than being here alone, watching late-night Argentinian football highlights on Eurosport, jeans unbuckled and eyes narrowing, microwaved pasta stains running down my shirt.

I look at the Commissioner. Her still taut skin is glowing under the yellow sitting room light. A few strands of her auburn-grey hair have escaped from the rigid sweep-across style she favours for professional events. The rebel locks are now curling around her eyes on either side.

'Come on Richard, next question?' She takes a deep swig from the beer can. 'Where's your stamina?'

She laughs and pulls up a chair on which to rest her feet. Black tights cling to her calves and the curvature of her feet. The citizens and journalists and cameramen are gone now, and so too is the ossified grin. She starts to talk about her time at university.

'I used to frighten the boys when I got angry debating politics. They didn't know I was putting on an act to get their attention – maybe I played the role too well!'

I find myself listening.

'When I graduated, it must have been 1983, no, 1982, I had no idea that I'd end up in Brussels. I guess I imagined being one of those popular local mayors, you know, 'woman of the people', Amsterdam maybe. No-one could have called me distant *then*.'

I feel tenderness for her plight but am ill-equipped to express it.

Half an hour later we are in my bedroom. Mental exhaustion, a good dose of physical fatigue and four cans of beer have led us slowly down the corridor, burning the last bridges of formality along the way. A series of words flash through my mind. Appropriate conduct. Professional distance. Keep a work-life balance. The word-emitting arsehole opens and closes again.

We cross the threshold into my room, the last bastion of me, Richard Cohen, spokesperson to the Commissioner. I feel an immense weight binding us together, the gravitational pull of hours and hours spent alone, in the office, on the road, a litany of sarcasm and working lunches.

'So is it how you imagined?' I ask, watching her eyes pan across the room. She makes to reply but stops as a ringing noise cuts through the room. I detect a shade of something in her eyes – irritation, offence, both? – before realising that the ringing is coming from my pocket.

'Eleni?' I call into the receiver. I make instinctively for the corridor, but think better of it. I rest my eyes on the window next to the Commissioner.

'Richard, is this a bad time to call you?' Eleni asks. She sounds restless. I look at my watch: 00:45. Only the beautiful can afford such an imposition. Unfortunately I do not have the integrity to resist it.

'No worries,' I say after a second. 'What's up? Apart from *you* of course!'

'I need to talk to someone about the Commissioner,' she starts, oblivious to the very fact of my joke, let alone its comic merits. There is a coin sitting on my desk – I've had it for so long that I can no longer remember which currency it is or how I procured it. I grab it with my free hand and massage it between my fingers as she talks.

'The thing is,' Eleni says, 'I think she's being unfair with me. She's constantly criticising my work. I wanted to talk to you because you know her so well.'

'Yeah, I guess so,' I reply, shifting my eyes onto the Commissioner. She has her arms folded and appears to have twigged the nature of the call. 'Look Eleni,' I say, relishing the sound of her name coming out of my mouth, 'It's a difficult job, especially at the beginning. It happens to all of us that sometimes you feel … unappreciated'.

I sneak a glance at the Commissioner. She raises her eyebrows at me.

'But it doesn't happen to you,' Eleni replies. 'The Commissioner respects you, she doesn't talk down to you like she does to me.' For a moment I actually reflect on what she has said. Then I remember that she is waiting for me to reply.

'Just chill. You've only been there for a few months. If you keep working hard you'll see that the Commissioner is pretty fair.'

Our eyes meet again and she mouths the word *pretty*?

'And believe me, we all make mistakes. We just have to bounce back from them.'

I lay the coin back down on the desk. Whether my advice has any merit to it is now immaterial. I have become the word-arsehole. As the call peters out, my thoughts are elsewhere.

'So, Richard, do you often discuss the way I treat my staff at one in the morning?' the Commissioner asks. 'You were very diplomatic, I must add, but I guess it helps that she's so young, so pretty?'

'She means nothing to me.' My voice comes out deeper than expected.

A silence ensues and my words reverberate back off the walls, crying out for explanation. I think about backtracking but cannot work out how. I look at her but my embarrassment is not reflected back. She who can hold the gaze of a hundred journalists. She starts to move around the room, pausing on every strewn garment and CD piled up against the wall. Then she turns back towards me.

'Everything's such a mess,' I say, but she shakes her head and continues her exploration of the room. Now she's standing at my desk, running her hand over scraps of paper like the priceless exhibits of a historical archive. She picks up a scruffy page from the floor and holds it closer to her eyes to make out the pencilled text. She moves towards me, and reads out slowly:

I am blinded by the beauty of your olive eyes,
When they speak, they drown out your words,
Pray mercy oh eyes of thee (?)/ thine

She raises her eyes towards me, her lips parting towards a question.

'It's for you,' I say, deepening my voice again, looking her head on this time.

Truth, logic, plans are a world away. It is the thrill of saying it that draws the words out of my mouth, and sends them surging towards her watery, green-brown, possibly olive-tinged eyes.

The Commissioner pulls me up against her and our lips meet. I am shocked to find nothing pulling me in the other direction. My neurotic days spent judging myself and others with such deep scrutiny have yielded no moral compass, and not a single conclusion to draw upon now. We kiss effortlessly, our hands gripping each other like a place they have always known, even at night.

'Richard,' she whispers. 'Take my clothes off.'

07:20

A haze of morning sun cuts through the curtains. Her eyes open and I catch my reflection in them. Still me. Still the same grumbling passenger, poised at the precipice of another day. She rolls out from the bedclothes and starts to dress. I lie still for a moment, just to be sure of the motion around me. Time is elapsing, deadlines are expiring, emails are accumulating, and the midday press conference is approaching. I stumble towards the bathroom, and a piece of paper sticks to the underside of my foot. *I am blinded by the beauty of your olive eyes.* I scrunch the sheet into a tight ball. The mirror greets me with a smile.

Sybille Regout

A Belgian Wedding Picture

The story of Anne-Laure

Weddings. Obviously, you can only adore them. Weddings are what you dream about, aren't they? A happy ending. You used to fantasise about weddings like you did about marshmallows: as a swirl of whiteness. White dresses, white flowers, white-toothed smiles ... They are white, and sweet. So sweet. Of course you love weddings.

But all the same ... The first weddings were exciting, but that feeling doesn't last. Suddenly you turn twenty seven, you've got ten weddings a year and they all look alike. They really do. It seems like all newly-weds have been offered the same wedding package by the same company. Same venues, same food, same guests ... It's like living the same day again and again.

Besides, it's never your wedding.

Anyway, you know the awkward feeling when you enter a room alone? When you stand there, on your own, scanning the crowd for familiar faces? Everyone around you sees that you are lonely and friendless. They pity you, and you feel like an idiot. I've had a few of these moments, and they are really embarrassing. I try to avoid them at all costs.

So today, the price is sharing a car with Christine and Robert.

Don't get me wrong: Christine is my best friend, we've known each other for ages. I love Christine and Robert, I really do. But sharing a car with them is a desperate move. Why not their bedroom while I'm at it?

'So, Robert,' I venture, in order to break the ice. 'Your little sister, getting married. What a change, huh?'

Robert is driving but his right hand isn't on the gearstick, it's on Christine's knee, and I mean 'knee' in a rather general sense. I guess Robert doesn't realise I can see him even though he cannot see me. He probably hasn't ridden in the back for a while. Besides, I have to admit I can't actually *see* him: my view is obstructed by the two front seats and I can only guess what his hand is stroking by the angle of his arm. Knee. Focus on knee.

'Yeah, well, it's not like we haven't seen it coming,' Robert replies.

'But still, she's so *young* …'

'Christine was twenty four when we got married.'

'Right.' There is a brief silence, broken only by the purr of the engine and the sound of Robert's hand on the fabric of Christine's dress. His overstretched spine looks like a gothic vault, and I can spot every vertebra of his neck as if it were an exoskeleton. What did she ever see in him?

'Ahem.' I clear my throat in the hope he will notice me. 'Robert, do you mind putting the heating on? I'm a little cold.'

'There, I'll do it love,' Christine says, speaking for the first time. Robert looks at her adoringly, while she moves a nonchalant finger towards the dashboard. Damn. There's always an awkward moment when you remove your hand from somebody's 'knee' and you don't know if you are really going to put it back there. I was hoping for such a moment. But I guess Robert and Christine don't have those moments anymore.

'It's *so* nice of them to have invited me,' I continue.

'Yeah, well, my sister knows you pretty well,' says Robert.

'But still. She doesn't know me *that* well. Come to think of it, I might even be closer to the groom ... He's a good friend of my flatmates.' Robert doesn't budge. I turn towards Christine, but she doesn't reply. Though I can't see it, I know she is fidgeting with her wedding ring, engagement ring, and all the other rings that do not have a specific function, except to provide her with handy fidgeting material.

Wait, she's fidgeting? This can't be good ...

'Actually, Anne-Laure, there is something Robert and I wanted to tell you,' she says.

Her anxious gaze catches mine in the mirror. 'There are ... going to be some changes for us,' she starts. Then she stays silent, exchanging a long, hesitant look with her husband.

'Changes?' I ask.

Christine reaches for Robert's hand, *finally* removing it from her thigh area. Bless you, Christine, you really are a friend. Oh, and Robert ... He's looking as proud as a rooster. It must be something to do with him.

'Oh, congratulations Robert!' I squeal. 'So you got that position in Geneva! That's wonderful, you've been looking forward to it for so long ...'

Robert laughs nervously, in three short and punctuated jolts. It's just enough to make me understand I'm wrong. Or stupid. You never know with him.

'No it's not that,' he says. 'We are expecting.'

The unlikely image of Robert with an inflated belly reaches me before I can actually make sense of what he is saying.

'Oh,' I say. 'A baby.'

For a moment I don't speak, unable to find anything to say. They don't speak either. The silence lasts and lasts. Oh, wait. That coy smile of hers. *I* have to speak; she is waiting for my reaction.

'Oh! Congratulations! What amazing news!' I say, a bit too late to sound genuine.

'Yes, we were planning to keep it a secret until Robert's sister got back from her honeymoon ... No point in overshadowing her big day, is there? But since you were here, we thought ... I mean, it seemed appropriate ...'

'Oh, no, I mean, yes, you were right to tell me! I'm not going to tell them.'

'It's a girl,' Robert adds.

'Oh, good! Well, congratulations!'

'Yes,' he smiles. 'And she's already three days ahead!'

'Ahead?'

'Big,' Christine specifies. 'She's three days bigger than the average three-month-old foetus.'

'Oh, good!'

'Not that it worries me, but they keep on switching the due date, it's a bit annoying, you know, it will either be on the twenty-ninth or on the second.'

'Of what?'

'March,' she says.

'April,' he says.

'Well, the twenty-ninth of March or the second of April,' she replies. And they exchange a blissful, tender gaze again. 'But please don't say anything!' she continues. 'We've only just started to tell people. In fact, you're one of the first ones to know.'

'I'm so glad.' I frown. Not because of what she says, but because Robert has placed his hand on Christine's 'knee' again. Wait ... Now I can see it's not her knee. It's her belly.

☼

Christine and Robert had to be with the bride in order to enter the church right before she does, so I've taken a seat next to Louise. Louise! The idea struck me as soon as I entered the church: why didn't I think of Louise for the car ride? It's so ridiculous, I mean, she's my flatmate.

I spotted her immediately: she's not easy to miss. She is wearing a yellow cocktail dress with tangerine shoes. Her wavy hair is set loose, with a few strands tucked away in golden pins to make it look dressier. Every man is looking at her already.

Wouldn't it be easy to be her? This morning, it took me about an hour to choose my dress. I washed, I waxed, I plucked, I pondered. Louise, on the other hand, woke up and was stunning already. Does she even know how lucky she is? Every day, she wakes up with thick blonde hair that doesn't need taming; timid blue eyes surrounded by a ring of oversized eyelashes; and she is slim, really slim. All she needs to do is put some clothes on. No make-up, no hairdo, no foraging in the closet to find those jeans that do not make her look fat. Because nothing will make Louise look fat. And now she is displaying just how effortlessly chic she is. Just like everything here, she is on display. I wonder why she is still single.

'How has your day been so far?' she asks.

'Fine,' I answer. 'You know, eventless. Woke up, got a lift from Christine and Robert … Nothing to report. Christine is still Christine.' Damn. Did I give anything away? There's no way she knows about the baby already. 'How was *your* day?' I add quickly.

'It was good,' she answers giddily. 'You know, eventless. Nothing to talk about. Raph is still Raph.'

'I see.'

Raph is my other flatmate. He's also with the groom at the moment. In fact, he's the best man. Isn't that sexy? *Best Man.* As in, 'Oh, my boyfriend is the *Best Man*.' That would be nice, to be able to say your boyfriend is the best man. Not that Raph is my boyfriend or anything. I mean, that would be nice too, but I don't think he

97

would ever consider it. There's not a chance, with all those single Louise-like girls around him. I should feel lucky just sharing a flat with him. Some girls would kill to be able to swoon over his empty bottle of deodorant. Sometimes I wish he would look at me and see something different, but I've seen his past girlfriends and I am nothing like them. He deserves a real woman. I am more of a drinking buddy.

So, as I was saying, everything here is on display. Your invitation says, 'the bride and the groom would like to invite you to share the joy of their union'. But they don't want to *share* the joy. They want to *display* the joy. Actually, delete *joy*. Replace it with: *smug enjoyment of having found someone while some of your guests remain single*. As if their lives were successful compared to mine. Who invented wedding parties, anyway? Whoever thought it was a good idea? I mean, would you show the keys to your new house to a homeless person? Well, what happens here is that they are not only showing it. They are asking their parents for a costly party in order to celebrate it. Not that I would compare a husband to a home, apart from the fact that both offer you some security. Maybe I could compare a boyfriend to a rented home, and a husband to a mortgage. I wonder what Raph would say about it.

Oh, here comes the groom. He's walking towards the aisle with his mother. You can't miss her: she's the one with the oversized diamond brooch. Then there are the bride's mother and the groom's father. The siblings, Christine and Robert. The bridesmaids and ushers. Ah, there's Raph! I could recognise his face from a hundred miles away. 'Look, there's Raph,' I whisper to Louise. 'Saw him,' she replies. Wait, is there mist in her eyes? What, like she's about to cry? 'Oh come on, Louise. You don't even know them,' I shush her. 'I can't help it,' she replies.

And here comes the bride: Robert's little sister, arm in arm with Robert's father. *Little* sister. Can you imagine? She's twenty four, and she actually looks twenty two. Where is the world heading to if twenty-six-year-old grooms marry twenty-four-year-old brides? Is twenty seven too late? But that's not the worst of it. The worst is yet to come. By that, I mean the reception.

☼

I know that the reception is supposed to be the dreamiest part of the whole wedding thing. Cocktail dresses, hats, shoes, bags, tuxedos, waiters, champagne, canapés … Shall I go on? But then there is the whole mixing and mingling part. You never really have time to engage in a conversation. You need to greet someone, make small talk, move on, greet someone else. It's so easy for couples, they move together. Whenever they are on their own, they don't look sad. They look adorable. I, on the other hand, have to find people to talk to. People who greet me, make small talk and move on to greet other people. I have to fight to not have those alone-and-searching-for-familiar-faces moments. It's so exhausting. I would much rather be at home, watching a DVD with Raph and Louise. I wouldn't follow the movie of course, I would be far more focused on the three of us sitting on the same sofa. Raph would sit on the far end of the couch so he could throw an arm over the backrest. Louise would take off her shoes and stretch out her feet like a cat. Sometimes she would sit on the floor, using our legs to support her back. We would sit around the screen as one sits around a fireplace: for the light, for the warmth. It would be so cosy.

But instead I'm standing here on the wet grass, with high heels and only Louise. Where is that champagne glass I was promised? Oh, wet grass, yes. You might be wondering about that. You see, this is a country wedding. All weddings are country weddings nowadays.

For a start, it can't really be called *the country*, as it is taking place within a thirty minute radius of Brussels. But who would attend your wedding if it was too far from the city? The newly-weds are not country people, and have no intention of becoming countrified. But somehow, it doesn't bother them. In their wildest dreams, they would have married in a castle. They visited a few places, asked for a quote, checked with the parents and eventually compromised on a farm. A lovely farm made of old bricks. The dinner takes place in the barn, and the reception in the gardens. A subtle waft of pig suggests intensive farming in the area. Belgian weddings all look the same: white tables, black tuxedos, green grass and brown mud. It's as if these colours were breeding. Rain leads to green, which leads to mud, and somehow the tuxedos and the wedding tables get squeezed into the frame. Not that it actually matters: none of this would make it into the final wedding picture anyway. No, we will be sent a black and white shot of a black tux, white dress and greyish faces: not enough light, too many clouds. We are in Belgium, after all.

'Congratulations!' Louise whispers to Christine.

'Sssshhh!' Christine replies, her face beaming. 'It's still a secret out there.' So much for being the first to know.

My heart leaps with a heavy thud. I can see Raph's neck, he is right next to us, speaking to another guy. It's true that necks aren't particularly sexy in general, but his neck *is*. In fact, it's not only his neck. It's the curl of his brown chocolate hair above it, and the wide aperture of his shoulders below it. It's a package, I like all of it. Every time I see his neck, my knees feel weak and my hands get sweaty.

'Raph!' I call. He turns his face towards me – oh, the muscles of his neck! Then gives me a quick wink, but doesn't move. It feels awkward. Now I feel like I must move. I excuse myself, but Christine and Louise are still in raptures over the supposedly-secret tummy bump, so I doubt they even hear me.

'Hi Raph,' I say.

'Hi, Annie.' Did you notice he calls me Annie? Other people just call me Anne-Lo. 'Annie, have you met my friend Justinien?'

'No, you haven't,' Justinien replies.

'Well, that is surprising!' Raph continues. 'Juste, this is my flatmate Anne-Laure. She's a good friend of Christine's. Justinien studied engineering with me.'

'Oh, I know Christine!' says Justinien.

'Who doesn't?' I reply.

'Anyways, you two should get along. In many ways, you remind me of each other. Hey, do you want champagne? I spotted a waiter over there …' Before I can speak, Raph is gone. I look at the sturdy, plain face of the man standing in front of me. 'Thanks Raph,' I mumble. An engineer. God, he looks dull.

'So, Justinien. You studied engineering?'

'Yeah,' he smirks. 'Although it's not as if I actually enjoyed it …'

'Who does?' I reply, suddenly conscious that I've said roughly the same thing in the two responses I've given him.

'Did you study engineering as well?' he asks.

'Me? God, no. I studied management.'

'Ah.' He smiles, as if he wanted to say, 'I see.' But he just smiles.

'Soooo …' I ponder. 'Do you work in engineering?'

'Kind of,' he says. 'And you? Do you work in management?' He's got a really flat nose. His eyes are ok, but his nose is really flat.

'Errr … Yes,' I reply. 'I'm working in project management.'

'Oh, you're a project manager then?'

'Not exactly. I work with a project manager.'

'Oh, good.'

'Yeah.'

There is a short pause.

'So, you're Raph's flatmate,' he says. Ah, familiar ground.

'Yeah. We're sharing a flat. And you? How do you know him?'

'I studied engineering with him.'

'Oh, that's right,' I reply. 'Errrmh, and I guess you're a friend of the groom, then?'

'Yeah. We all studied engineering together.'

'Ah. Yes. You're all engineers.'

'Indeed. There's a lot of us over here. Like that guy just there. And that one. We were all in the same class,' Justinien says.

'Only guys, huh? No girls in that class?'

'Look, we're engineers,' he laughs loudly, and I kind of laugh too, but politely. 'I know it's pretty clichéd. The groom over here is the exception,' he continues. 'But all the others are single.' I gather that this little statement includes him.

Lord Help Me.

Then suddenly, out of nowhere, the divine sound of an angel. 'I told you you'd get along,' Raph says, and I almost choke myself with my own saliva. He's got two glasses of champagne, but offers one to Louise (who, it appears, has finally detached herself from Christine's belly), and takes a sip from the other one.

'There's one good thing about weddings,' Justinien says. 'It's the free champagne.'

'It's not even champagne. It's sparkling wine,' I reply. 'Presented in champagne flutes just to trick us.'

Justinien laughs and beckons over a waiter.

'Do you always treat waiters like that?' Louise asks, her shy, flickering eyes forgiving the rudeness of her comment.

'No,' he answers. 'At some point I'll ask for their mobile numbers so I can call them and not have to move any more than necessary.'

This time, it's my turn to laugh. He might be plain, but at least he's funny. I guess that's why Raph thought we'd get along. Wait, does he consider me plain? Why would he think I'd be getting along with an engineer with a flat nose?

'I was just telling your friend Anne-Laure,' Justinien says, 'about how we engineers are doomed to singlehood.'

'Oh, that's nice,' Raph answers. 'Though not all engineers are part of this equation.'

'What, are you no longer single?' Justinien asks.

Raph chuckles.

'Look at the groom,' he answers.

And they both laugh again. What is so funny about that? Louise tries to laugh too, but I think it's only a group thing. You know, whenever someone yawns, and you feel like yawning as well ... Louise always feels like laughing as well.

The waiter eventually reaches us, but there is only one glass left on his plate. Oh Lord. Competition. Justinien looks at the glass, then at me, then at the glass again. No way. This glass is mine. The waiter looks at both of us, hesitating. But before he can take a decision, Christine demonstratively snatches it from us all. She stares at us, one by one – Louise, Raph, me, Justinien. She pretends to take a sip as she turns away from us, and I follow her.

'What are you doing?' I say. 'Alcohol?'

'Relax,' she replies. 'I'm not drinking. I'm only pretending.'

'What?'

'Come on, Anne-Laure! Robert's family is here ... Taunting me with this 'it's your third year of marriage' kind of thing. They are watching to see if I drink booze at my sister-in-law's wedding. Can't you see that? Because if I don't, then I'm pregnant.'

'But you are!'

'Precisely. But they don't need to know that yet.' She looks at me quizzically, her large, brown eyes glowing with that pregnant glare. I heard it's because pregnant women puke all morning; it makes their eyes glow. Then she reaches Robert's side.

'Robert, love,' she whispers, almost biting the side of his ear. 'You're telling your family that *you* will be driving on the way back, aren't you?'

How does she manage to make *that* sentence sound dirty?

'Wait,' I say. 'You said *you* would be driving.'

'Exactly. Because I'm not drinking,' she replies. 'But I am allowed to drink, am I not, love?' she babbles into Robert's ear again.

'Are you practising your baby talk?' I tease her.

'Shhhshshshhhh! What, are you crazy? Using that word with Robert's family around?' Her eyes are firing thunder.

Robert places a soothing hand around her waist, as if she were just going into labour.

'By the way, Christine,' he says. 'I don't mean to interrupt, but my great-great-aunt is over there and she wants to see you.' And just like that, they both glide away. Ah, here it is. My first searching-for-familiar-faces moment. I look around quickly - there's nobody I know. Plan B, go, go, go! I'm heading for the loo: I might come across an acquaintance on the way. You always come across acquaintances on the way to the loo.

☼

I don't meet anyone on the way. So I use the loo and wash my hands extensively afterwards, just to display the fact that I am washing my hands extensively after using the loo. As there still isn't anyone I know, I move on to Plan C: the bar. After all, I still haven't had that free glass of champagne, or sparkling wine, or whatever. And just as I reach for the bar, a familiar face turns towards me.

'Oh, Anne-Laure,' Justinien says. 'I was looking for you. Here is your glass.'

My glass? When did I ask him to get me a glass?

'Thank you,' I force myself to smile. 'What happened to your taking-the-waiter's-phone-number plan?'

'Ah, it was a joke.'

'Ah, I figured that too.'

'It's not always guaranteed,' he replies. 'Your friend Louise didn't get it.'

I imagine Louise's helpless lashes fluttering over her delicate blue eyes and I giggle.

'I am serious,' he says. 'She now thinks I'm gay.'

'Haha! As if.' Oh, no. Why, why, why? Why did you say that, Anne-Laure? Now he's going to think that you are hitting on him. Or at least checking his relationship status. But why would I need to check that? For a start, I'm not interested. And secondly, it's quite clear that he's single.

'It doesn't matter,' he replies. 'She's taken.'

'What, Louise? She's not taken!'

'She's not?' he asks. 'It's weird, I could have sworn that she was.'

'Why would you think that?' I ask, but I know full well the answer: because girls like Louise are always taken.

'Oh, it's just … I had the feeling that … But I might have been wrong. I mean, you're her flatmate, right? You would know about it.'

I take a sip from the champagne glass. Another waiter passes by with small *feuilletés*, but as usual, targets the parental circles and forgets about the rest of us.

'Anyway,' Justinien says. 'Are you a friend of the groom or a friend of the bride? I couldn't figure that out.'

'Both,' I say. 'Well, both, and neither of them, really. She is Christine's sister-in-law, and he is Raph's best friend. Anyway, it's *so* nice of them to have invited me.'

'Well, at least you know them both,' he smiles. 'I've never seen the bride in my life. I'm just glad she's wearing white. I wouldn't have recognised her.'

'Yes, brides tend to do that. Wear white.'

'Have you ever been to this place before?' he asks. I shake my head.

'I have,' he continues. 'And there is a strategic spot, right over there, near that small staircase. It looks like a redundant space, but some of the waiters actually use it to make an alternative approach to the crowd.'

'Eeeerm … Thanks.'

'You're welcome. Anyway, that's where I'm heading.'

I quickly look around, and realise another looking-for-familiar-faces moment is well on its way. So I decide to follow him. After all, it's always good to get along with your boyfriend's friends. Even when your boyfriend isn't your boyfriend yet.

☼

Thank God the reception is over. I am with Louise now, eating fries at the nearest *fritkot* with some of the other guests. We make an incongruous crowd, the girls in cocktail dresses and the men in three-piece suits mixing with the usual customers: chubby men whose hairy chests are covered with tank tops and grease spots. But no one is surprised, it's what a Saturday night looks like out here. You see, only close friends are invited to the wedding dinner. I am not a close friend, and therefore I am buying fries at the nearest place, waiting for a decent time to come back to the venue.

I love fries.

Louise has stolen a little plastic fork and is nibbling from my plate. But this nibbling thing is worse than if she hadn't been eating at all. She is pressing every fry she steals against a napkin in order to absorb the grease. After five bites, she declares she is full. 'I ate soooo much at the reception,' she says. It's true that she spent a brief part of her afternoon in Justinien's strategic spot and ate some of the mini fruit salads.

'So, this Justinien,' she tells me. 'He's a fascinating guy, don't you think?'

'Why would I think that?' I ask.

'Well, just, you know. With his CV, he could have gotten any job on the market. He could have made a lot of money, just like Raph. But he decided to build wells in Madagascar instead.'

'Wells in Madagascar?' Oh my, I can't form a mental image of *that*. His engineer's body in a charity t-shirt and his flat nose covered with sun cream.

'Yes, didn't he tell you?' she asks. 'After university, he went to do some voluntary work for six months – something of a tradition in his family. But he really liked it. So he didn't know whether to carry on, or get a high-flying job ... In the end he made the decision by flipping a coin. Yeah, a coin! He's now working for an NGO in Brussels. I'm surprised he hasn't told you. I mean, you've spent quite some time alone together ...'

Now I don't like the sound of *that.*

'Louise, it isn't what it seems,' I say quickly. 'We didn't talk that much. In fact, he asked me about you all the time ... Like, if you were single and all.'

'Oh really? Because Raph's been briefing him about *you* non-stop.'

'I don't know why Raph would do that.'

'Come on, Anne-Lo,' she says. 'We both know you've been single for about a year now.'

'And so have you,' I add. Louise looks at me, looks at my fries, looks away, and then at me again.

'Yes,' she says. But her tone rings false.

'You're not single!' I squeal.

'Yes, yes, I am,' she answers.

'Who is it? Come on, tell me, who is it?'

'I'm not *with* someone,' she replies firmly. She pauses, choosing her words. 'I'm just ... attracted to someone.'

107

'Oooooh … I see.' Now that sounds more like her. 'Do I know him?'

'You do.' Her lips quiver. The night is a little cold. She steals another of my fries and tortures it against her napkin. 'But I can't tell you who it is, just in case, you know … in case he doesn't love me back.'

'Louise, who couldn't love you back?' I answer. 'Look at you! You outshine them all.' She smiles. Vanity. That's what is going to lose her. Her eyes look up from the fries and she asks cautiously, 'Can you keep a secret?'

☼

Back to the party. I have put Plan B into action one more time, but now people are going to think that I am incontinent, and I know full well that I shouldn't abuse Plan C, otherwise people are going to think I'm an alcoholic. Instead I ask for a glass of whisky and coke with no whisky. So basically, a glass of coke, in a whisky and coke glass. Yes, I'm sure, thank you; and I hand it to Christine.

'Here Christine, a whisky and coke for you,' I almost shout. She raises it to her nose, checks it is alcohol-free, smiles and answers as loudly as she can.

'Thank you for the whisky and coke, Anne-Lo. I am so glad you got me one, though I have to admit: I've had one too many.'

'Well, that makes two of us,' I answer. But that's not true either. I am so sober.

'Ah, Annie!' Raph calls me. His curls are casting spells over his godlike face. The muscles around his smile! I wish he didn't smile like that.

'Raph. How was the speech?' I ask.

'It was good. Good! People laughed a lot. Especially when I pulled out this little engineering anecdote …'

'Oh great,' I interrupt.

'Are you ok, Annie?' he asks. 'You look a little down.'

'No, I'm fine. A little tired, that's all.'

'Good. Well, I'm here to lead everyone to the dance floor; it's going to be the first dance.'

'Ok. I'll see you later.'

I hate the first dance! It's the worst part. I don't want to do this. I follow the crowd like a lemming on its way to the edge of the cliff. I am standing next to Christine and Robert. Bad move, I realise. They will be tempted to join the dance. I need to find someone who is single. Here! Louise. I am standing next to Louise.

The first notes reveal that it's a waltz. Didn't waltzes disappear with the last century? But then I'm not that surprised: Robert's family looks like the waltz-dancing kind. The bride is gliding happily in her father's arms, her smile so broad that her face could break in two. Next to me, Louise is hugging herself, swinging from side to side. Then the bride's father hands her over to the groom, and everybody applauds. Please! Why would you applaud that symbol? What happened to feminism? And the bride looks so blissful, so blissful. Robert and Christine join the waltz, Christine demonstratively shifting her centre of gravity backwards, holding her belly forth. And other couples, too. In fact, half of the onlookers have gone to the dance floor. I am not one of them.

Wait, it's Raph. It's Raph, and he is walking towards me. I smile – I shouldn't smile! I am so obvious. He smiles, too, but nervously. He looks so handsome. My hands are sweaty again – he will notice. It's terrible! And here he is, right in front of me.

'Louise, do you want to dance?' he asks her. Her lips stretch over from one cheek to the other. 'Of course I do,' she answers. And there they are, flying away, as if it were the most natural thing in the world. His hand is on her waist, her hand is on his shoulder, and they look each other *in the eye*. As if nothing else existed.

Earlier tonight, when Louise spoke that name … It was so cruel. So obvious! How would it have been possible for me *not* to see it coming? 'Do you think he likes me too?' she asked. 'I don't know,' I answered. But I knew. I knew he did. And even now, seeing them dance in each other's arms … I have never seen *that* smile on his face. Never. Not for anyone. Of course! Of course he likes her back.

This is horrible.

'Champagne?' a voice asks me.

I don't even need to look up to know who it is.

'I hate first dances,' I tell him.

'I can see that,' he says. 'Are you OK?'

I still don't look at him. I feel like I have been stabbed in the chest. I can't really breathe. I hear Justinien talking, but I can't grasp the meaning of his words. Perhaps … If I keep quiet long enough, maybe he will go away.

But he doesn't. Instead, I feel myself gently taken by the arm, and led outside the room. Outside, into the bitter air. The night is really, really cold. He makes me sit on a chair. A splashing sound surprises me. I look up: he has just thrown away the champagne from my glass, and is pouring water into it from a bottle left on a nearby table.

'Here,' he says. 'You should drink a little water.'

I sip from the glass.

'Are you feeling better?' he asks. I nod. 'It's very common, you know, a little bit of claustrophobia,' he continues. 'Fresh air and water, that's the best remedy I know.'

'Is it how they do it in Madagascar?' I ask.

'Oh,' he smiles. 'So Raph has briefed you about me as well.'

I freeze again. I can't face the sound of his name.

'That's not funny,' I say.

'Not feeling better then?' he asks. I don't answer. 'Right. Shall I call Christine? She can take you home if you want.'

'No, no. I'm going to stay here for a moment,' I reply. I breathe in, and out, and in, and out. He takes another chair and sits next to me. He doesn't try to speak. What was I thinking? Why on Earth did I believe Raph would be interested in me? It was Louise. I've known it all along. And the thought of going back to my flat – to *our* flat – to *their* flat. I hate it. I breathe in, and out, and in again.

Then I notice Justinien is just like a Belgian wedding picture: a black tuxedo on a white chair, in the middle of the green grass and brown mud. Except it's the night, and everything looks black and white. I laugh, a little private laugh.

'I thought it wasn't funny,' he says.

'Sorry,' I reply. 'It's been a weird night.'

'That's OK', he says. 'How are you feeling?'

'I don't want to go back in there,' I answer.

'That's also OK.' His face is poorly lit; from this angle, his nose doesn't look so flat. I don't think he looks plain anymore. I rest my back against the cool fabric of the chair.

'Can I ask you a personal question?' I say.

'Sure.'

'Did you really gamble your future on the toss of a coin?'

He hesitates. Somewhere, in the distance, the pig smell is making a subtle comeback.

'Only my job,' he answers. 'I don't think that that is the most important aspect of my future.'

'Not the most important part?' I answer. 'Then what is?'

'Yeah, it's hard to figure that out.'

'Yes,' I reply. I look at him. It *has* been a weird night. He took me out of that room. I knew Raph wouldn't have done that. Raph wouldn't have cared enough. 'But your job … Isn't it important?'

'Plenty of things are important,' he continues.

I say, 'You didn't really gamble it on a coin toss'.

'Not really. But sometimes, heads or tails … It helps.'

☼

The party is over. I am in the car, back with Christine and Robert. Christine is driving, as she said she would. Robert is a little drunk.

'You didn't have to drink them all,' she says reproachfully.

'You handed me the drinks,' he says.

'Of course I did. But that doesn't mean you shouldn't have known your own limits.' Her voice is as sharp as a knife. She is angry.

'Christine,' he drunkenly mumbles. 'Your hormonal crisis is really starting to get on my nerves.'

'My crisis? *My* crisis?' she suddenly shouts. '*I* am the one who is pregnant. *I* am the one who is going to have this baby. How will you like my hormonal crisis then? How will you take care of another human being if you can't take care of yourself?'

'Now that's going too far, Christine darling,' he says.

She looks at the road. 'I know, love.'

None of us speak for the rest of the drive. I pretend to have fallen asleep. Robert's hand is on Christine's 'knee' again, and she isn't so angry anymore. I know they will be fine. I am slowly running my fingertips over the edges of a coin. I smile. Weddings. Obviously, you can only adore them.

☼

Dany G. Zuwen

Eight Days

The story of D'Amour

Day One

Awakened by thirst, I face the room; grey tones, tight walls – it assaults me.

It's dark outside, and if I didn't know any better I'd think it was early in the morning. But here in Brussels, I'd be foolish to guess the time by the colour of the sky. A quick glance at the alarm clock beamed against the ceiling tells me it's three in the morning. No use trying to go back to sleep; I'd just lie on my back like an idiot, watching the unceasing parade of red seconds until the alarm goes off.

As I try to get out of bed, I notice I can't move or feel my hand. I follow my arm like a thread, which leads me under Clémence. Taking the greatest care not to wake her, I manage to free my hand and sit on the end of the bed, massaging the sleeping limb. I look back over my shoulder at her body, rising and falling as she breathes.

There was a time when I found that motion comforting, a time when I would have smiled and felt overwhelmed by happiness. But for what feels like an eternity, I've been lying next to a person for whom I hold nothing but contempt, resentment, and perhaps even hatred.

As soon as my feet touch the soft, once bright-white carpet of our tiny studio, I *wake* up. I study the room, from the pile of unwashed clothes scattered around wooden boards that used to form a rudimentary wardrobe, to the ridiculous kitchenette where a single sink is home to a tonne of unwashed dishes. The dark, heavy curtains form an impenetrable shield set in place by some cruel god to whom my despair must be entertaining. The sheets smell as if they need to be cleaned. Actually, the whole room has a rancid stench to it. It reeks of passionless sex, an act that pleasures neither of us, but has become some kind of ritual, like glue, the only thing still holding us together.

How did we get this low; how did I get here?

I decide.

It ends. Right here, right now.

Day Two

Summer looks more like autumn as I sit on a worn-out steel bench, sheltered from the strong and wet wind by a glass-framed bus stop.

I think about yesterday's conversation with Clémence. I guess I should call it a monologue. Once I finished tripping over my own words, she stood there and stared at me. Unable to withstand her half-shocked, half-angry look, I hurried out. When I got back, Clémence was gone.

☼

Soon, none of what happened matters. My heart pumps faster, rushing blood through my capillaries at an incredible speed. Every part of me feels alive now that I have *her* in my field of vision.

From the bus stop I see her exiting her building on Rue du Noyer, closing the front door behind her, and leaning against the wall to avoid getting soaked by the rain. I wonder if her entering my life had anything to do with my relationship's decline. I doubt it. Clémence was a mistake. She was a sinking ship, and I shackled myself to her.

When the next bus arrives, the wind gives way to a breeze, reminding me that although I don't like living in the city, I love the earthy smell of the asphalt after a good old Belgian rain.

While I'm lost in internal monologues, the girl frowns angrily as only busy people do, and pounds the keys on her phone. She hasn't seen the bus, the one she always takes, and my last if I want to be on time. Since I first saw her six months ago, I haven't gone to work without her.

As soon as the doors open I rush inside, battling to be among the first to enter. An old lady shoots me a dark look when our shoulders collide. 'Does your shame have no limits?' asks her glare.

I reach the driver's booth and lean in as close as I can against the assault screen, point at the girl, and ask him to blow the horn. He doesn't understand what I mean. I know his type; he's one of those guys who considers himself someone's brother because their ancestors lived on the same continent millennia ago. Once again, I lean in, invoking an informal tone. After all, we're buddies.

'Donne un coup de klaxon mon frère, elle va rater son bus!' I nod towards the distracted girl. He seems to understand this language much better.

The girl from Rue du Noyer, centre of my fantasies for the last six months, is startled by the short, aggressive noise. When she sees the vehicle, she grabs the bag at her feet and flies towards me.

Before she arrives, the driver turns to me and winks. I force a smile before heading to the back. There's no need for her to know why the driver waited. I watch her rushing towards the bus, and wonder how a pair of heels can reflect so much light on such a dismal day. The raindrops caressing her forehead are like a final layer of polish on the most refined of sculptures. I look at my barely ironed shirt, and grab an inconspicuous seat near the back. What could I have to say to someone like her?

She is speaking to the driver now. Unsurprisingly enough, the Moroccan traitor points at me. *It's fine, relax. She's just a girl, for God's sake.*

She's right next to me. Either she's fast or it's that relativity thing, the whole 'time flies when you have a deadline –' *Come on man, concentrate.*

'Thanks,' she says. 'If I'd missed this bus – let's just say my boss would've killed me.'

She smells incredible. *Stop that. Talk back to her. Say something funny, girls like funny, everybody knows that much.*

'It's all right. No one likes to miss their bus.'

The girl grins politely, and her smile, however fake, sends sparks running through my body. I consider getting up for her; after all, what do girls like most after humour, if not chivalry? I stay seated a moment too long, and soon the window of opportunity vanishes. A tall, blond guy with a tan too brown to be natural rises and points at his empty seat with a crouched back, imitating a fancy restaurant waiter, saying he's getting off at the next stop anyway and that her heels look uncomfortable. She flashes a somewhat embarrassed smile and shakes her head. Someone jumps in the seat, giving the blond guy an excuse to stay standing – between her and me.

You're the sun that I need to bloom, the wind to help me fly, the sleep I crave to dream. You look like a wonderful, unsteady baby dragonfly, standing on a dewy, green blade of grass under spring's morning sunshine.

That's what I long to whisper in her ear, where silver earrings shimmer in the form of water droplets. However, like so often in my life, I decide to keep that sentence at the state of a thought once I realise that I'd basically be calling her a wet insect.

The blond guy looks down at me over his shoulder with a triumphant look. He readjusts his shiny tie, wipes invisible dust off his wide shoulders, and turns towards her, starting what I can only imagine to be a funnier conversation.

I can still smell her perfume. A touch of lavender.

Day Three

I slept like the dead last night.

Clémence was everything wrong with my life; I can make something out of myself now. I know it. If only I had a chance with the beauty from Rue du Noyer … *Stop kidding yourself man, what do you think? Have you seen her? You work in a barbershop for heaven's sake, what do you think she does for a living? You are funny though … I'm sure if girls could see your thoughts they would be on their knees – with laughter.*

I'm late to the bus stop. I don't even bother looking across the street. I fear I'll see yesterday's playboy kissing her goodbye. I rush to the bus that's already pulling out, waving at the driver. Fortunately, it's my ally from yesterday. I thank him with a nod as I enter, flashing my ticket. There she is, right in front of me, looking back.

'I saved a spot for you,' she says.

Her r's have a sweet sound to them, slightly rolled. Not awkwardly obvious like Africans, but not funny like the French either. Perhaps a subtle Russian accent, or even Danish. Oh well, there's no point in guessing; her accent could be Martian for all I know.

'Thank you,' I say.

'You're welcome.'

Part of me wants to ask her about the tanned businessman, part of me knows how dumb that would sound. I decide against it, and start scrutinising her instead.

Her long, white skirt and blouse contrast with the grey bus interior, and emphasise the paleness of her skin. She looks almost unreal. Being this close to her eyes, I'm swallowed up by two holes filled with strange colours. It's as if God, unwilling to provide such a unique creature with a common trait, created a brand new shade just for her.

'You don't speak much.'

Great, she noticed. *What did you think? A deaf person on the other side of the city would have noticed. It's okay, relax. She kept a seat for you, the least you can do is bless her with a normal, plain conversation like only you can make them.*

I can't stop looking at her, spellbound by every aspect of her body, drawn by the mauve scent. Something made visible by a low neckline catches my eye. It shines like a sun between two mountains that are her breasts. Hanging at the end of a necklace so thin it's barely visible, reflecting a wandering sunray, a hand-engraved silver coin rises and falls as she breathes.

I soon realise how close to her chest I've leaned in pursuit of this strange treasure, and I feel a sudden rush of blood to my face. She, on the other hand, keeps displaying this angelic, to-be-damned-for smile.

Day Four

She's in the same spot as yesterday. Next to her, the tanned guy is looking in the opposite direction, a gloomy look on his face. Perhaps they're not in the middle of the sensual conversation I envisioned. She removes the folder from the seat opposite.

'How are you?' Is it me or is my voice trembling? *Don't worry about it, just listen to her answer. You don't want to ask her to repeat the first thing she says.*

'I'm fine, how about you?'

I smile and reassure her that I'm doing fine as well. My tanned rival throws a deadly look at her, then at me, and I hope it's because she turned him down before my entrance.

'I'm sorry, I didn't even ask your name.'

Congratulations, finally something useful to ask, says her playful gaze before she answers in a soft and unique word. 'Aislin.'

I was expecting something more Russian, but is she even Russian and if she is, is there such a thing as a Russian name? *Do not ask that question.*

'It's beautiful,' I say before I realise how predictable that answer is. I want to take it back, find something original to say, but it's too late.

'Where are you from?'

'Don't you think you should tell me your name first?

Well, she's bound to find out one way or another. 'D'Amour.'

'Isn't that 'love' in French?'

'Err … Literally, it means 'of love'. I didn't choose it,' I add rapidly. I sound like I'm trying to justify my existence, but she doesn't seem to notice or care.

'It's original. I like it.'

'I think my parents wanted to make sure I wouldn't introduce myself to many girls.'

'Don't say that! It shows how much they must love each other.' Her voice shakes a little as if she were remembering something sad about her own parents. I can't picture her having problems like the rest of us.

The next stop is Schuman. That's where we both get off, but she'll stay above ground while I head down to the metro.

Ask her something. Anything.

'Doesn't your name have a meaning?'

'It means Dream,' she says, looking puzzled by my inquiry.

'It's very accurate.'

I meant to say that in my mind. Having lowered my gaze, I'm afraid to lift it up to gage her reaction. First I try the tanned guy. He's smiling as if to say, 'that's the stupidest pick-up line I've ever heard', and he's right. When I look at her, she's still smiling. Or maybe she's laughing at me. I don't care.

I let her out first as we exit the bus, and I try not to trail my eyes along her legs and stare at her ... Realising how miserably I've failed, I draw my eyes upwards only to find hers peering back at me over her shoulder. How fortunate that she can't see me blush.

'Well, D'Amour,' she says in her wicked tone, trying to pronounce it à la French, which sounds exquisite, 'I'll see you tomorrow morning'.

'Yes, of cour – Can I have your number?'

She seems as surprised as I am, and her smile disappears for a moment. As far as I can remember, including my early years, I've never wanted so desperately to be an ant. She smiles, reaches for her wallet, and takes out a piece of paper. Is she really going to give me her business card? I guess that would be a polite way of telling me to keep dreaming. She puts her wallet back in the bag, and fishes out a pen. She scribbles on the back of the card before handing it to me. As I take it, right when our fingers meet, two things strike me; her hands are softer than a chick's downy feathers, and compared to hers, the colour of my skin must be the reason why people call us black.

EIGHT DAYS

Day Five

It's raining today. Again. I envy the freedom of the water drops, fooling around, flying, falling, hitting the transparent walls of the bus-stop, splitting, and falling some more; living such a short but intense life, no worries, no bills to pay, no languages to learn, no low-paying, dead-end jobs to suffer through – that must be the dream.

I can't take my eyes off 103 Rue du Noyer. A few times the doors fly apart, an umbrella pops open, people jump out, others get in – she doesn't appear.

The bus arrives, people get on, more get out, all try to run faster than the falling water, and still no sign of her. My stomach gets heavier by the minute. My friend the Moroccan throws a sad smile at me, as if he can feel my pain, and I wave at him, distracted. Our seats are free. I was hoping she'd be there, that maybe she'd taken the bus one stop earlier.

I take my phone out and dial her number. I hang up before it can even ring. The idea of another man hits me, Rolex watch on the bedside table, Ralph Lauren shirt folded on a chair nearby. I can almost hear his rough morning voice spilling out of the receiver, and it sickens me. I consider saving her seat, but what would I use in place of her nice, important-looking folder with an EU logo on it? I can imagine the look the old lady from two days ago would give me if she came to sit only to find a pair of scissors occupying the seat.

It has barely started, but to my mind one thing is already clear – today is a write-off.

Day Six

Her hoarse voice surprised me, but then I realised that for someone not working, it must have been quite early. The urge to hang up there and then was hard to fight, but my number was displayed. She'd find out who had been calling.

Sitting on my couch – soon to be my bed – watching the rain as it pounds on the windows, dripping in silence, I replay the conversation in my head.

'Hello?'

'Hey. It's me, D'Amour. You know, the guy from –'

'I remember you. How are you?'

'Fine. I'm sorry to wake you, I was worried.'

'Worried?'

'Yes. You know …'

'No. I don't.'

'Well, you didn't come for two days.'

'Oh! That.'

'Yes. Sorry. I wanted to make sure everything was fine.'

'Don't apologise. It's sweet of you.'

'I'll let you get back to sleep.'

'I thought you wanted to make sure everything was fine.'

'Yes.'

'So …'

'So? Oh! Right. Are you all right?'

'No. Not really.'

'Why? … I mean, what's wrong?'

A laugh. 'Don't worry, I'm not dying. I was coming down with something for the past couple of days, maybe the flu. The doctor recommended a few days off, I thought I could use the rest.'

'Sorry to hear that. Are you eating properly?'

Silence.

'Are you laughing?'

'Yes, a little. Don't take it the wrong way, but that was an unexpected question. Even from you.'

'It's important to eat well when you're ill.'

'I know, it's just …'

'What?'

'It's something I'd expect to hear from my mother.'

'Sorry.'

'You don't have to apologise for everything, you know …'

'Sor – Are you laughing again?'

'Sorry!'

'Don't worry about it. Well, I should let you rest.'

'Are you trying to get rid of me?'

'No, not at all, but I don't want to take too much of your time.'

'You're strange.'

'Oh!'

'It's a good thing. Well, strange may not be the best word for it, but English is not my mother tongue. Sometimes I can't find the right words.'

'What is your mother tongue?'

'Is it important?'

'No, just curious.'

'Is it all you want to know?'

'No, but if I asked you all I want to know, the batteries would die long before I finished.'

'You're funny.'

'Are you sure of the word this time?'

'Yes.'

'Good.'

'So, why did you ask the driver to wait for me the other day?'

'Because otherwise you would've missed the bus.'

'Come on, be serious.'

'I am.'

'Okay. So what if I'd missed my bus?'

'Then I wouldn't have seen you.'

Through the phone, a smile. 'Why is that important?'

'Because, I like you.'

'You like me?'

'Yes! … What's wrong?'

'I didn't expect you to say that.'

'Why?'

'Because, you've been looking at me for six months without even speaking to me once.'

'It's the phone.'

'The phone?'

'Yes. I'm … not very skilful when it comes to talking to girls. Especially if I like them.'

'Is it easier over the phone?'

'Looks like it.'

'I should have given you my number long ago, then.'

'Is that a good thing?'

'How could that be a bad thing?'

'Eat with me.'

'Come again?'

'I mean, let me have dinner with you. Sorry, what I mean is, let me cook you a good meal, that way I'll be sure that you're eating properly.'

'You can cook?'

'My friends say I'm pretty good. I'll make you my best recipe … if you accept.'

'What is it?'

'You'll see.'

'Okay. When?'

'Tomorrow. After work.'

'What time is that?'

'Six o'clock, is that okay?'

'Great. What do you want me to get?'

'Some rest. I'll take care of everything else. Do you like wine?'

'Yes, I do.'

'I better get going, this is the last metro if I don't want to be late. What's your address?'

'Is this your number?'

'It is.'

'I'll text it to you, then.'

'Great. See you tomorrow. Get better.'

'See you tomorrow. Thanks for checking up on me.'

Day Seven

Everything is almost ready. I put the rice on in a separate pot, give the sauce a stir, and appreciate the subtle aromas of garlic, sweet onions and red peppers, well-measured saffron, and the beautiful, yellowish colour of the mixture. Lowering the heat, I take note of the time before joining Aislin in the living room. Her apartment, angles everywhere, immaculate walls, bursts of colour here and there, is huge for one person.

'Mmmmh! It smells great,' she says. I notice she has already set the table.

'I'm sorry it takes this long, but I'm a slow cook.'

'Don't worry. You know, when you said you'd take care of everything, I didn't think you'd go to such trouble.'

'You deserve it.'

She smiles and slouches in front of the TV.

'Come sit with me.' She pats the free space to her right. I obey. She grabs the remote and fades in some music after muting the television. The volume is almost non-existent, but I still recognise *Für Elise*.

'So, what do you do for a living?' I ask her before she gets the idea first. I'll find a way to keep the conversation on her, and as soon as she asks about me, I'll make sure there is an emergency in the kitchen.

'I work for the European Commission.'

'Do you like what you do?'

'It's boring but otherwise all right. Pays the bills.'

I look around. It must pay more than the bills. I say nothing.

'A penny for your thoughts?' she asks and then adds, 'I've always liked that expression.'

To hell with it, why not just ask her. My uncle always told me that you shouldn't undersell yourself to a woman, otherwise she'll think you're weak. But my uncle also taught me that a man should have a woman for every night of the week – in every city of the country ...

I want to have the confidence my uncle was talking about, but every object here feels like a rope tightening around my neck. I feel like a dirty cotton sock in her drawer of nicely-folded-all-silk underwear.

'Do you like me?'

She looks up, smiles at first, then probably sees how lost I am. She erases her smile. 'I'm starting to.'

'Why?'

'Do I need a reason?'

I sigh.

She flashes me a little smile. 'You don't talk much, and when you do, you say something unexpected. You surprise me, and I don't get surprised very often.'

I glance at my watch; the rice is ready.

☼

'Oh my God! This is the best meal I've ever had.'

'Thank you,' I say, clasping my palms together.

'No! Thank *you*.' She closes her eyes, licking her bottom lip to remove an excess of the yellow sauce. This small gesture turns me on in so many ways that it can't be healthy. I lower my gaze, fearing she can read it. She goes on complimenting my dish and I have to say, it makes me feel damn good. Clémence couldn't appreciate a tasty meal. With her, eating was a matter of sustenance.

'You see what I meant, you're full of surprises.' She looks straight into my eyes.

I want to get up, kiss her, caress her, run my fingers along her legs, pin her against the wall while –

'You're drifting again,' she reminds me, the light dancing on her smile. I beam back.

'Are you up for dessert?'

'There's dessert?' She looks impressed.

☼

When she puts the spoon in her mouth, she closes her eyes again, and moans with pleasure.

'What is this?' she asks, separating out the words.

'Mango, apple, and banana mousse infused with lemongrass and topped with biscuit crumbs. You like it?'

'Are you kidding? I *love* it. Did you make it?'

'No, it made itself. Of course I did.' I'm starting to relax around her, but my bodily temperature is still rising.

'This is heaven,' she says, pausing after each word again, before setting aside the empty cup and caressing her stomach. It's incredible how the simplest action from her seems erotic to my eyes. I start gathering up the dishes, trying to hide how happy her compliments have made me.

'Leave it, come on. Dance with me. We'll clear up later.'

She snatches my hand and drags me to the stereo where she taps a few times on the docked Ipod. She rests her head on my chest. At first, we dance to the sound of a thick silence interrupted only by my heart pounding like a herd of elephants, her hands around my neck, mine weighing on her hips. We realise she forgot to push the play button. After exchanging a laugh and awkward smiles, she does just that. I'm lost in the cocktail of odours: her perfume and shampoo.

'Is this wise for someone in your condition?' My breathing is heavy, and I feel like iron heated to melting point. I tighten my grip.

'Do I look sick to you?' She raises her head from my chest to look into my eyes, our noses inches apart. We're so close that I can smell the lemongrass on her breath, and I'm so far gone I can't answer. We're still in the same position, our feet barely circling the floor.

The song finally starts, and it doesn't take me long to recognise it – Marvin Gaye, *Sexual Healing*.

From the look on her face, she wasn't expecting it either, probably a random song from a shuffled playlist. A nervous laugh breaks between us, but rapidly things become serious again.

The gap between us closes and our bodies meet. First, her breasts press against my chest, soft and firm. Next, our lips clasp together. The kiss is a tad salty, very sweet, and almost as slow as our dance. Our embrace intensifies, and it gets harder and harder for me to keep my hands to myself.

She drags me to the bedroom and Marvin fades, leaving the stage to other artists that I don't care to listen to. In the room, our lips still locked together, my left hand caresses her back while my right flies everywhere, from her buttocks to her hair, combing it with my fingers. Soon, her shirt is gone. We're on the bed, and I leave her mouth for her neck. She removes my shirt. Then our trousers join the other clothes on the floor, and my hand reaches for her back, battling with the clasp of her bra.

I distance myself from her to look at her slender body as it lies there, expecting me. The possibilities are infinite, the whole world within reach. I return to her, using my tongue to feel the salty softness of her body. The down between her breasts makes her chest feel like it's covered in peach skin. My hand goes up and down her thigh, grabbing it at times, pulling her as close as possible.

When at last she's free of her clothing, when the only item left on her body is the roughly circular, light-reflecting coin, I keep going down, my hands circling, enveloping, and massaging her breasts. I kiss her navel before trailing my tongue past her pelvis, along a pencil-thin line of almost white hair.

As my mouth encloses the junction of her legs, she arches her back and gasps. Her hand running along my hairless head freezes. She closes her legs without consideration for my trapped head while small shivers run through her body. She pulls me up, flips me over, and I feel her hand as she guides me in.

The power I feel inside me has no equal but the beauty I see whenever I can pry my eyes open. She moves with unnatural grace, sliding, undulating, her eyes closed, my hands resting on her hips, following her furious rhythm.

We've been at this carnal dance for a timeless moment. We're covered in sweat and I'm on top of her. My hips accelerate to exhaustion. Her eyes lock onto mine and noises, animal cries, escape from our joined bodies. And for a stolen moment in time, we create our own, true happiness.

Moments later, calmer and satiated, I feel complete. I've become a careless raindrop – I'm free. Today, my life starts anew.

Day Eight

Awakened by thirst, I face the room; white shades, infinite space.

I leave Aislin and roam around the flat. I lie on the sofa, comfortable, cosy, smooth. I slide my feet through the soft carpet fibres. I peek at the spotless bathroom, at the spacious cupboards.

In the kitchen, under the mountain of undone dishes, a dishwasher, Whirlpool. A microwave oven that works. A huge fridge – full.

☼

When I come back to bed, I find myself before a scene of such beauty and cruelty that I can only hope to be trapped inside a dream.

Aislin lies on the bed with her head in the shadow of the lunar light. Every other part of her magnificent body is lit, the chest where her nipples rise fiercely against the freshness of the night, her curvaceous and slender legs. The moon casts a glowing, grey colour and gives the scene a sense of unreality.

The coin around her neck reflects a stronger light, a white glow against the grey, moon-painted background. I catch my reflection in the body-length mirror next to the wardrobe. Despite the moonlight, all I can see is an outline. I rise onto my tiptoes, trying to fill the void between my negligible figure and this towering ceiling. I stare into the space where my face should be, but can barely make out a thing. My features felt strong and delineated when she was touching them. Now they have faded back to nothing.

When I turn to look back at Aislin, as my eyes water, as I claw at my chest, I know – one day, perhaps tomorrow, or the day after, or the year after that, just as it did with Clémence, the cycle will repeat itself.

One day, I'll wake up filled with resentment and powerlessness, and I'll wonder what I'm doing next to Aislin.

☼

Enrique Medarde

Alternative Businesses
The Story of Adam

As I promised my good friend Viktor, I'm going to put down on paper all the events that led to the rise of the new Underground King in Brussels, so they can be remembered and retold in years to come. I take on this task without regret, for the means of doing so are more available to me than to any of the other people involved.

It will, of course, be a personal view. After all, any story we tell is filtered by our own prejudices and how we see the world.

It all began when I decided to leave my hometown and wander the world. My family was a well-connected one in Valladolid. My father owned one of the biggest and most prestigious law firms in the whole city, and a modern – yet old-fashioned-looking – villa in the suburbs. My mother was a housewife, she neither had nor wanted a job, but she was involved in many social projects, mostly to project a healthy façade to the community and high society acquaintances. They may sound like a good family, but my father was obsessed with his work and my mother never took a real interest in anything. She let me do what I wanted, often saying *of*

course and meaning *whatever*. To please my eager father, I pursued studies in Law and achieved good marks in my exams, emerging as one of the preeminent students on my course. My father was exultant to see me do so well, as it laid the foundations for me entering the family firm and becoming his associate and future owner of the company. But the more I saw of this world, the harder it became for me to hide my growing disgust with the corporate excess and paternalism that ruled it. I realised that I wanted to walk my own path, not one that others had laid for me. So instead of entering my father's firm, I stuffed some clothes and things that I couldn't leave behind into my backpack, and boarded a train out of town, unsure of where my future lay, but certain that it required me to leave Valladolid and my family behind.

☼

I found myself in Paris. I had heard good things about the City of Light, and was eager to get to know it, especially the Louvre Museum. As it turned out, the city was spectacular, but they didn't let me into the museum. At the time I had yet to learn French, but it being close to Spanish I could make out the meaning of *fétidité* and *vagabond*. The little money I had was soon gone, so I had to resort to begging in the metro, where my harmonica - one of my mother's castaways - turned out to be a very valuable asset. I knew some lively tunes and, as I started to pick up some French, I could compliment the ladies and make witty remarks about them to the men, so I soon became very proficient at making a living out of this.

However, some of the old-timers grew jealous of how I, a newcomer, was doing so well for himself. I was often mugged, and my favourite spots to perform at the metro stations were usually taken before I got there. The handful of acquaintances I had made tried to look out for me, warning me away from trouble and teaching me how to wield a knife in my defence. I grew to love these kindly folk, and their city, but others were making my existence there impossible – and I thought about leaving again.

Unable to decide, I resorted to one of the most ancient decision-making tools: the toss of a coin. And that's how I ended up on the first train out of Gare du Nord. It took me north, to Brussels, and everything that the city held in store for me.

☼

When I got to Brussels I had neither money nor friends, and remembering how an acquaintance in Paris had had plenty of both – until he got caught – I decided to enter the drug business. In the beginning it's no easy ride, I have to admit, you are at permanent risk of being busted by the police or beaten up by other dealers. The money you make is not so great, either. But it got me started and made me some very useful contacts.

Vasken the Northerner was one of them. He owned a shady sort of company called *Alternative Businesses*, where I was soon taken into employment. The company hired people for the most varied jobs imaginable, from corner-boys selling drugs on the streets, to the thugs protecting them, from forensics – for more delicate jobs – to mercenaries. If you required a service that wasn't considered legal or you just didn't want the police to know about it, *Alternative Businesses* could provide it at a reasonable cost.

After some time, I took what was apparently a very simple job. I had to pick up a box, guard it for a couple of days, maybe three, without opening it, and then return it to the person who had first given it to me. I accepted the task, and the following morning a nervous-looking man approached me and told me he had something for me. He gave me a wooden box with carvings on the sides and the top. It was the length of my arm from shoulder to wrist, and not wider than my palm. He said he would return soon. But a week later I was still in possession of the box, and had no idea what to do with it. I tried to contact Vasken, but he wasn't in town, so I was stuck with the stupid box. I made the promise to myself that if no one claimed it over the next three days, I would open it. Then, I went to sleep.

Eight hours later, I was running like a madman down Rue Haute.

I had spent the night in Parc Royal – something I usually don't do, but I was feeling regal – and got up refreshed and ready for a new day. Suddenly, as I was making instant coffee on my camping stove, I heard somebody sneaking up behind me. When you've lived on the streets for a while, you know better than to turn and greet the stranger, so I picked up the wooden box and started to run. I heard a man cursing behind me, and a couple of gunshots that fortunately missed me. I looked back and saw a bald man brandishing a baseball bat. The other guy with the gun reminded me of a B-movie action hero; he was wearing round sunglasses and a ponytail.

I sped down Rue Royale towards the looming Palais de Justice and took a right turn onto Grand Sablon. They continued to follow me, but for the moment I was having no trouble keeping them at a distance, even though I could feel my lungs starting to cry in pain. Luckily we were no longer in the park, where they could risk a couple of gunshots. That's something I've learnt about the bottom part of society: you are seldom taken notice of by the others.

I knew that if I could make it to the vicinity of Gare du Midi I would be safe. I sped down the street avoiding cars and old women by inches, jumping over trash bags and nearly bumping into furniture on display. The cobblestones are not the best surface to run on, but as it happened, it hadn't rained for almost a week, so the street was not as slippery as usual. About halfway down Rue Haute I started to recognise some of the faces that were looking back at me with amazement. It revived my hopes and breathed new strength into my limbs. I risked a glance back, and saw that my pursuers were still hot on my heels. But they had lost a bit more ground, mostly thanks to the help of the people who knew me and were throwing trash and other assorted objects at their feet.

I stumbled out of Rue Haute onto Porte de Hal and saw the entrance to the metro. Hoping to shake off the two guys, I flew down the entrance to the station but, as I was crossing it towards the other side of the Petite Ceinture, I heard the tram coming. I changed directions and rushed down the second set of escalators, along an empty corridor, and through the closing doors of the metro carriage. My pursuers rushed up, hitting the doors, but the train was already pulling away and I sighed in relief. They shouted and kicked innocent bins and benches, and I danced a little jig. Then I collapsed on an empty seat, and waited for my breath to return.

Seeing as I was on the metro, I decided to go pay a visit to one of my acquaintances - Nikos the Greek. Despite Nikos' preoccupation with selling things, I trusted him completely. He owned a junk store in Saint-Josse called *The Little Corner Shop*, but I swear I've looked for that corner every time I've been there and have never ever found it. Nikos was as incongruous to look at as the shop itself. He was a tall, slender Greek with clothes as black as his raven hair, and yet his disposition was sunny and open. As he was always talking, it seemed that he never listened to anything people said, but those who had met him knew better than to assume that. I never grasped how he managed to listen while talking, I've tried it myself – it's a useful trait to have, after all – but I've never managed.

'Hi, Nikos, how's the day been treating you?' I said. His smile was contagious.

'Not bad, Adam, not bad. I made a few big money sales this morning, that's why you caught me in a good mood. But where are my manners today? I didn't even offer you anything to drink, excuse me, my friend.' He clapped towards the back room.

'You look tired,' he continued. 'Have you been running? You are sweating and stinking up my store.'

'Yeah, I've been running *a lot*, and all because of this stupid wooden box.' I showed it to him. 'Actually, this is one of the reasons I came to talk to you.'

Suddenly, there was someone behind me and I spun round, startled.

'Adam, this is Viktor; he's been working here for some time. He's my right-hand man, he takes care of the chores I entrust him with, from making the tea to ... let's say, more complicated assignments.'

Well, whoever this Viktor was, he could be as silent as a cat. I hadn't heard a thing, and he was standing no more than half a metre away from me. His skin was neither pale nor healthily tanned. Greyish, one could say. He looked fierce and could probably kill a wolf with his bare hands, but his voice was high-pitched, and that made him seem kind of inoffensive. But something told me that he used that as a façade – and often.

Nikos told him to bring a couple of Jupilers and before I realised, Viktor had disappeared.

'Well' – Nikos started again – 'tell me about that box of yours and why you are stinking up my office.'

'You know that some time ago I started working for *Alternative Businesses*. A few days ago I got this job to hold onto a box for some time and then return it. The usual, you know. But the guy who gave me the box didn't come back. Instead, a pair of thugs have been chasing me all morning. And they had guns. *Guns*, Nikos, this isn't Baltimore, we don't do guns!'

'Hmm, I see. So it's clear they mean business. And you don't know them? Or the guy that hired you? That may be important, see, I usually try to find out everything I can about the people I do business with. For example, this business yesterday. He was a fancy-looking guy who -'

'Nikos! I'm not here to listen to your business stories!'

'Shut up and learn, my friend. Well, this guy was fancy-looking, as I was saying. But something about him made me realise that he was not all that he seemed. His watch was one of those plastic ones you can find for five euros and he looked uncomfortable in his shoes, as if they were borrowed. So I didn't lend him the money he was asking for, knowing that he wouldn't return it.'

'What does that have to do with me?'

'It's the details, my friend, the *details*. You gotta learn how to pay attention to them.'

Nikos and his bar-stool advice, I thought.

'Thanks,' Nikos said, and I noticed the two beers that had materialised on the table. Viktor was nowhere to be seen.

'I think it'd be a good idea if we opened the box and took a peek inside,' Nikos suggested.

So I took the box and put it on the table. I opened it and Nikos jumped out of his seat.

'Sweet mother of the Holy Lamb, Adam! Do you know what that is?'

'C'mon, look at my face.' I was probably wearing the expression of a kid watching *Citizen Kane*.

'*This*,' he said, 'is the Underground King's sceptre.'

'Hm-hmm.' My expression was unchanged.

'Quite some time ago there was a King who ruled us, the homeless, the wanderers, the peddlers, the junk dealers ... those living at the margins of society. But this is not the place to teach you history, I'll take you to a more suitable place. Just know for the moment that the contents of that box, which you, my friend, are carrying, represent the most important discovery for our people for a long, long time.'

I started to chuckle, but his humourless expression stopped me in my tracks. Nikos wrote something down on a piece of paper and handed it to me.

'Go to this address, it's a safe house I have for emergencies. At the door just say *Thessaloniki* and someone will let you in. I'll make some calls and then come to you.'

'Thanks Nikos,' I said, accepting his offer with no further word.

I reached out for the empty beer can to throw it away, but it was not there. This Viktor was a ghost, I swear. I never got used to how stealthy he was.

☼

I spent six hours in that house and when the faded floral wallpaper was starting to drive me insane, Viktor arrived. He told me Nikos had arranged a meeting with some important people and that we were required to be there soon.

The apartment was close to La Bourse, one of those places which exist primarily to serve as a meeting point. We walked past it and towards De Brouckère, passing by all those kebab shops everyone seems to be in on a Saturday night before the metro re-opens. I still knew where I was when we walked down Boulevard Emile Jacqmain, but I was suddenly lost when we turned into a maze of little streets, full of dodgy-looking night shops and decadent strip-clubs. After a while we approached an office building with an off-brown *frontis* that looked like the façade of an old Greek temple, decorated with images of powerful gods and naked women. Viktor rang an intercom sandwiched between *inDesign* and *Flowers International*. We were buzzed in.

Nikos was waiting for us at the elevator and guided us through a decaying wooden double door. Beyond those doors was an immense and strangely under-furnished hall. There was a desk at the end and a small table around which four people were seated on high-backed sofas, sipping tea from old mugs, and smoking in silence. I felt strangely out of place – the four figures looked very old, a weighty mixture of wisdom and tiredness in their eyes.

'Adam, my friend, let me introduce you to *The Concillium*.' Nikos started explaining. 'The contents of that box are crucial to our existence. Some time ago there was an Underground King, a ruler, someone we could rely on to arbitrate any problem, question or dispute. Before that time, it was every man for himself, we were scattered and disorganised. Then it was agreed that a ruler was needed for our survival. This goes back to the Middle Ages.'

'Do you really expect me to believe that?' I looked him square in the eyes.

'Well, that's your choice. I'm just telling you what has been and what we hope will come to be once again,' he said calmly.

'I shall be guided by you in this.' I had been wanting to use that sentence for years.

Nikos looked a bit puzzled, but he continued the story.

'We have some enemies. A former *Concillium* member known as Soft Toni was kicked out because of his extreme ideas, and he now wants to establish a tyranny and rule the Underground with an iron fist. He coats it with sweet words and beautiful ideas, but we know him; we know what the underlying purpose is. He formed a group called *The Fallen Knights*, or some nonsense like that. Anyway, that sceptre you're carrying is very important, as it will allow us to gain the upper hand and the support of the people to reclaim the throne, which has been empty for two hundred years.'

'What happened?' I asked.

'The Usurper happened.' Nikos almost spat out the words. 'He was the King's brother. The King was benevolent and

139

understanding; he knew the limits of power and how to wield it for the interests of the many. But his scheming brother coveted the royal sceptre, and the power that came with it. He devised a plan to get rid of the whole family and ascend to the throne himself. The sceptre has always been the symbol of power here in the Underworld, but the Usurper never laid hands on it. The King's youngest child managed to escape the carnage that followed, and took the Sceptre with him. Then, all traces of the child and the sceptre were lost. The slaughter cost the life of the King. The Usurper then proclaimed the throne to be his, but it came to be known that he was an imposter, and nobody accepted his claim. And so it goes that we have been King-less ever since. A seer, a very old woman who lived at the time, foresaw that a new King would arise when the Sceptre was found again.'

'I see why this sceptre is so important.' I stated the obvious.

'Exactly, and we are planning on -' He stopped suddenly, as the sound of heavy boots were heard on the other side of the door, along with cries and shouts.

'Soft Toni is coming!!' Viktor shouted as he entered the room – when had he left? – slamming the door closed behind him.

'Hurry! To the back exit!' one of the old men said, looking frightened and pointing towards a wall-mounted tapestry depicting the beheading of peasants on the steps of a town hall. Behind the hideous tapestry was a small hidden door that Nikos opened with a copper key. It revealed a passageway illuminated by a single light bulb and a barely distinguishable staircase at the far end, down which the old men and Nikos were already disappearing.

I looked back and saw Viktor standing there alone, defiant, like a modern Achilles.

'Run.' he ordered. 'I'll delay them for a while.'

'But they'll kill you!' I shouted.

'You don't know me yet,' he said, licking his lips and taking out a pair of nunchucks from somewhere in his clothes. 'Meet me at *A L'Imaige Nostre-Dame*. Nikos knows it.'

And so I burst through the door, pulled it closed and dashed down the stairs to safety.

☼

Nikos and I were back at the safe house, whose six hundred and thirty four flowers over a beige background I will never forget. I had told Nikos what Viktor had told me and we were making plans. Nikos knew that the situation could not go on indefinitely, that we could not run away from Soft Toni if the Kingdom was to emerge again.

He came to a decision to confront Soft Toni in a face-to-face knife fight, because apparently that was how disputes had been solved back when the Kingdom was prosperous and a settlement between the parties was impossible.

Nikos took a knife and started swinging it around in a totally amateurish way. In a knife fight you don't cut, you stab. At least if you are planning on winning. I knew that from my days in Paris, where I had seen too many of those fights, and had narrowly avoided several of my own. I relayed the basic techniques that my Paris acquaintances had taught me, surprising Nikos with my one area of street-smart.

We left the apartment and got into Nikos' old Renault 11. He was very attached to that car, even though it was older than Belgium. It was bright red and the seats were ridden with holes, the interior smelled like cigarettes, after-shave and vodka, and only one of the headlights worked. Nikos started the car and after the engine revived itself from pneumonia, we were on our way to the bar to which Viktor had summoned us. We had to pass by Nikos' shop first, though. When we reached Rue Laeken, on the way towards the

Petite Ceinture, we were jolted forward in our seats. Someone had shunted us from behind. Nikos managed to keep control of the car, and swore under his breath.

'*Malaka!*' he shouted as the car barged into us for a second time.

He sped up. We were travelling down Rue Laeken at no less than ninety kilometres per hour. The shop signs became a blur and pedestrians threw themselves back to the safety of the curb. Nikos was mumbling in Greek and I clung to my seat. The Petite Ceinture was quite close already, and the crew in the other car knew that. They also knew that they could not risk gunshots on such a big avenue, so they started shooting at that moment, with amazing dedication. Their accuracy, thank God, was not as impressive and they managed to hit neither us nor the tyres, so we finally made it to Boulevard du Roi Albert II in one piece.

Nikos took the ninety-degree turn as if he were Portuguese, and zigzagged between the other cars. Luckily it wasn't rush hour, so there was *some* space to squeeze the car through, but my heart has never raced as fast as it did during those minutes. I could see the faces of our pursuers and they looked familiar. They were the same guys who had chased me through the Marolles, the Bald Man and the Ponytailed Movie Hero. I didn't know how we were going to lose them in that piece of junk Nikos was driving, but I looked at him and he was obviously waiting for something, looking through the window to my right. I only saw a big queue of cars. We emerged from another tunnel at lightning speed and, without warning, Nikos turned the steering wheel. I swore at the top of my voice and looked to my right at the line of cars that was speeding towards us as the light turned green. My swearing turned into a girlish scream.

But we had made it. We were not dead.

We heard a crash behind us: it was the other car. That was what Nikos had been waiting for. A traffic light to turn green and – only just – enough time to put the line of cars between ourselves and our pursuers. At first I couldn't believe it and checked to see if I was okay. Then I scolded Nikos a little bit with a voice that sounded like my sister's. I didn't scold him much, though. After all, he *had* saved us. We changed plans and headed straight to *A L'Imaige Nostre-Dame*. After the chase Nikos feared that someone would be waiting for us at the shop. The bar should be safe, he told me, almost no one knows of its existence.

How can a bar be almost unknown, I thought to myself.

Suddenly, I wanted to be there.

Truly, one could never imagine a bar like this one. It was situated at the end of a very narrow *cul-de-sac* full of puddles of rain, badly illuminated and smelly. One could conceivably envisage it being a shisha bar or a shack where men bet on dogfights, but not an anciently decorated, happily-tended bar. It was run by two people, Alfa and The Wise Man, and it survived thanks to the handful of regular customers. The Wise Man served up a coffee for me and a Hoegaarden for Nikos, but I don't remember anyone placing the order. Viktor sat inconspicuously at a table in the corner, reading a newspaper and checking everything from top to bottom. We didn't sit with him for the moment; we were waiting for the other people to leave, just in case. Nikos took the opportunity to teach me about the Underground, the lost Kingdom and some laws and traditions that varied from those of Underground society in Paris. I could hardly believe that I had spent months there, in the midst of it, yet oblivious to its existence. Once the bar was empty, we sat with Viktor. His face was half purple and covered in cuts and abrasions from the fight with Soft Toni's people, but he was alive.

Viktor told us that when he had been beaten to a pulp and ready to face his death, Soft Toni himself had pulled his men back, and then approached.

'I am going to let you live, Viktor,' he whispered, 'but not because I like you, no, it's just so you can deliver a message to that happy-go-lucky boss of yours, Nikos the Greek'. 'Someday you won't be surrounded by your thugs and then the tale won't end with me on the floor and someone sitting on my back, mark my words,' Viktor had answered. 'Consider them marked, Viktor, but even though what I have in mind is different, it isn't as far away from the current situation as you think. There will be a fight, and that is the message I want you to deliver. I know I am faster and stronger than Nikos and that he is in no position to refuse, so I am offering a knife fight like those of old. Winner takes all.'

As it turned out, Nikos and Soft Toni's ideas were not so far apart. They both wanted to re-establish the Kingdom – though Toni was going to use it for his own benefit while Nikos wanted to revive the legacy of the last King – so they both reverted to the old traditions to settle the dispute.

It was to be a fight to the death, and I had seen Nikos use a knife. I looked at Viktor and he looked at me. He also knew how Nikos fought. So we decided to seize the opportunity and use the few hours we had until midnight, when the fight would take place, to teach Nikos what we knew. Viktor was as proficient with a knife as he was with nunchucks, so he would make the perfect teacher. I, meanwhile, would serve as a sparring partner. Alfa moved a couple of chairs and opened a trap door that was beneath them. We followed him and The Wise Man to the basement, where they had constructed a small refuge. I raised an eyebrow and The Wise Man just wiggled his fingers in front of his forehead by way of an answer. We moved the few pieces of furniture to make some room, and took two small pieces of wood to serve as training knives. I took one and threw the other to Nikos. He levelled the weapon at me and attacked, but I just grabbed his arm, pulled him in and stabbed downwards, to get at his neck. Alfa took his guitar and started playing old sea shanties. Viktor took the knife from Nikos, and the lesson began.

☆

Night had gradually fallen on Brussels.

We left *A L'Imaige Nostre-Dame* and walked slowly towards the Palais de Justice. Its massive structure and columns hovered over the city, reminding everyone that for every action there's a reaction, and if the action is illegal, you're not going to like the reaction.

In a sense, it was the perfect place for a knife fight. Justice would be done and the winner would take the throne. In reality, it was a practical choice as well. The building had been under repair for decades and the scaffolding had become just another decoration. No one went there at night, save some of the students who lived in the city and got together at *Place Poelaert* for some Jupilers before moving to the centre. There was a full moon and thus enough light to see without torches, which would have attracted unwanted attention to the building.

The news had spread, so a big crowd was waiting for us when we arrived. I held the box firmly as we paraded in front of them. There were some cheers and boos, but mostly the people had long faces and looked gravely at us. A shade of fear flashed across Nikos' face as we approached the end of the long *columnata*, where Soft Toni was waiting. They shook hands and looked each other in the eye. Viktor and I stared defiantly at Bald Man and Ponytailed Movie Hero. Toni and Nikos turned around to face the crowd and Soft Toni started talking, explaining that he and Nikos had reached an agreement whereby the winner of the knife fight would be the next Underground King. There were some shouts of disagreement, but then Nikos asked me for the box. He opened it and held the sceptre up in the air.

'Behold! For this is the Underground Sceptre, the one the old seer spoke of. Today, the new King will rise, and he will rise from a fight to the death, symbolising the end of the struggle, the infighting, the hatred of our brothers' – a collective gasp could be heard from the crowd. 'From this day a new era will begin, and if we manage to remember our history and thus prevent the errors that befell us in the past, it will last forever,' he finished in a roar, and the crowd went crazy.

People formed a big circle and Nikos and Soft Toni were ushered into it. Then, they went to opposite sides of the ring, where their people were waiting. Nikos stripped off his shirt and Viktor told him that he had prepared a surprise. He took a couple of items out of a canvas bag and explained that he had concocted some body paint the like of which the Celts and the Vikings had used in combat. He asked for my help and so Nikos sat on a small stool and we painted crooked lines, hands, dots and arrows across his face, torso and back. He looked impressive, painted in sky blue and white. Toni thought the same when we moved away, allowing Nikos to step inside the circle once more. His adversary did not seem as confident as before. He took his knife and made a cut along his palm, while looking arrogantly at Nikos. Viktor whispered in my ear that in some cultures the fighter cuts himself prior to a fight so that his blade has already tasted first blood. Nikos glanced at the sceptre in my hands, took a deep breath and turned to face his opponent.

Nikos and Soft Toni moved again towards the centre of the circle, standing some six metres apart. They started to prowl in circles, studying one another. It was soon obvious that Soft Toni was a better fighter than Nikos. He moved with more agility, almost in a feline way. Nikos held the knife as we had shown him, but his movements were slower. Soft Toni made the first move. He jumped forward with his arm extended, the knife ready to cut Nikos like butter. Nikos threw himself forward into the attack, avoiding the knife and stepping into Soft Toni's guard. He drove the knife into Toni's ribs, but Toni counter attacked with a head-butt that made Nikos' nose bleed. They pulled apart, breathing heavily and looking at each other. I realized that my knuckles were white, so tightly was I gripping the sceptre. The Palais was silent, all eyes fixed on the fight, and only the heavy breathing of the fighters could be heard. I looked at Viktor and he looked back at me with worry. The techniques we had taught Nikos seemed to have been well-learnt, but fights are long and we did not expect Nikos to be flawless. However, we were wrong on one count: the fight did not last long. After some careful glances and a bit more circling around, both Nikos and Soft Toni attacked. The attacks were perfect, both of them. With a feint, Nikos slashed open Soft Toni's neck, while Soft Toni had circumvented Nikos' left guard and lodged his knife into his opponent's side. Soft Toni fell to the floor, gasping for air, and was dead in seconds. Nikos, meanwhile, fell to his knees, with Soft Toni's knife protruding under his armpit. He knew he was going to be dead soon, but he managed, with our help, to stand up.

I placed the sceptre in his hand and he lifted it. With a last effort, he knelt again and handed the sceptre to Viktor.

'Long live the King,' he said, and then he was dead.

My friends, Bald Man and Ponytailed Movie Hero, didn't like that outcome, so they drew their weapons, but Viktor and I were expecting a reaction of the sort and we were ready. We unsheathed our own knives and the spectators made another circle. I saw that Viktor had disposed of Ponytailed Movie Hero in a flash, blocking his attack and stabbing him right in the heart, but Bald Man was giving me a little more trouble. The onlookers cheered and formed another circle around us.

He knew his way around a knife, and slashed me a few times. For the most part, they were superficial wounds, but people got excited at the sight of blood and started roaring. I paid no attention to them and waited for my opportunity.

I remembered a knife fight I once saw in Paris. One of the opponents had stumbled and almost fallen back, and the other had charged thoughtlessly towards him. He managed to kill the other guy, but I saw that his guard had been left open.

Bald Man and I were circling each other in one of those frequent pauses in combat; getting your breath back, weighing up options. I then pretended to trip over a hole in the ground and his eyes sparkled with murderous joy. His charge was so impetuous that my feint almost failed, but I managed to grab his right arm at the last moment with my left, and then I stabbed him in the wrist with all my strength. His hand went limp and let the knife fall. He screamed in pain. I smashed my fist into his face and his nose broke, spattering blood as he fell unconscious to the ground.

☼

Viktor and I were on the almost empty platform at Gare du Midi. I had stayed for Nikos' burial and Viktor's coronation ceremony, and for some time after to help him lay the foundations of his new kingdom. All those tasks had given me a sense of closure which I had not felt since leaving Valladolid, and brought Viktor and I very close – closer than I would have thought possible upon meeting him. I had the impression that my wandering days were over and I realised that I wanted to work as a lawyer, after all. I didn't yet know if I would take the position at my father's office or if I would pursue a career in politics, but either way I would try to help the Underground that I was sure existed in Valladolid, as it did in Brussels. Whatever the future, I sensed it was the right time to go back. My time in Brussels had come to an end, but the experiences had made me realise that knowing the law – ancient or new, clandestine or codified - could be used to help others. All those wanderers who need kindly faces to navigate through the backstreets and battles into which life has thrown them. The circle had closed; I had found what I was looking for when I left Valladolid a whole lifetime ago.

Viktor offered his hand but I hugged him instead. 'You know, Viktor, this doesn't mean that we won't be in touch,' I told him. 'You have my phone number and my parents' address in Valladolid, so we can write and call. And I will visit. Too many things have happened here to just forget about them. I will be there for you all.'

'I know,' he replied. 'But it's always sad when a friend leaves. And I thought you were staying to help me rebuild all this, to give me a hand, you know.'

'Yeah,' I said. 'I don't like goodbyes either, but it's my time to go, Viktor.'

'I know.' His voice had a resigned tone. 'Have a good trip, you ugly mug.'

'Have a good reign, you sneaky bastard.'

Ylenia Maitino

Colours of Brussels

The story of Anaïs

Where am I from? Different places.
How long am I gonna stay? I can't tell you exactly.
Where am I? Here for a while.

'Follow me,' she said.

That's how I first met Sarah, the skinny brunette in the design class. 'Where are we going?' I asked as we got into the metro carriage.

She didn't answer but took me to a small park in the suburbs. It was raining; still she wanted to lie down right in the middle of the park, on the green grass.

'Have you done this before?' she asked.

'Lying down in a park?'

'No, I mean taking a shower under the sky.'

Who hasn't? The rain was coming down heavily. 'Come here,' she pulled me down to rest next to her. Our arms brushed against each other for a few seconds. She closed her big green eyes and smiled.

We both decided to volunteer at a small art gallery in Sablon. I helped with the accounts, she helped to choose the paintings. We were post-graduate students, so we could only work the evening shift, which was twice a week, after six. Even though we were supposed to leave at eight, we would often stay on later to talk.

'Do you think Chagall believed in aliens?' she once asked while pointing at the reproduction of one of the Russian painter's masterpieces, hanging on the white wall in front of us.

'I think so ...'

'Really, you do?'

I paused and looked again at the painting. It was a faithful interpretation of *A ma femme* by a young Belgian artist. There was no gravity. People, animals, objects were all moving freely in the space around them.

'Yeah, I'm sure of it. Look at that bit. There are aliens, they can't be anything else. They all come from a different dimension. They look real, but they aren't. Like aliens.'

'What about you? Do you believe in aliens?' Sarah was sitting on the big armchair in the corner; her head was now resting on its inviting yellow pillow. The colour of energy, her favourite.

'Actually I do. I live with one: Julien, my little brother ...'

She laughed. Together with books, Julien was my most faithful friend. He would follow me everywhere, listen patiently to my stories and keep me company. I had never wanted to move away from home. But I had to. One year after my father's death, my mother got a new friend. I never forgave her for that. My father could not be replaced by anyone. Not in our house. Not that soon. I had to go somewhere else to finish my studies. I had to find a new home. Brussels welcomed me. Acquaintances were called friends and I had to make do with that. Until the day Julien showed up at my door to 'stay around for while' and I found myself in the company of a real friend again.

'What's he like?' Sarah asked.

'He's got green eyes, like you. He likes smoking joints.'

'Does he?'

'Yeah ... He likes to have one before bedtime; otherwise he gets insomnia and pretends to be a wolf howling at the moon.'

'He sounds funny.'

'He is. Also, he's obsessed with weird facts.'

'Like what?'

'Well, things like the fact that there are more chickens in the world than people, or that it's impossible to sneeze with your eyes open.'

She smiled at me, and spread her delicate arms over the backrest of the armchair.

Winter set in. Despite the cold, Sarah and I would walk long hours by the canal.

'So, has Mario asked for your number yet?' she asked.

'Who's Mario?'

'The Italian guy, he's in our video-lab. He's always staring at you.'

'Is he?'

'Come on, don't tell me you haven't noticed!'

'No, I haven't ...'

'He's cute ... not cute enough for you though.'

My cheeks flushed. I stopped and leaned over the railing along the canal. Sarah came up beside me and smiled. She never complained as much as I did about the dirty water or the grey sky. For her, nothing really had to be perfect to be fully enjoyed.

'Let's run!' she would challenge me, and for a while we would. Then we would fall back to our normal sluggish pace. Time was never an issue. It really wasn't.

☼

The first exam session came and went, and soon the colours started changing. We would spend entire weekends designing at mine. Outside, the rain was a silent lullaby. Inside, the music of Jacques Brel softly cradled us. Next to us, cross-legged on the floor, Julien would patiently apply himself to another thousand-piece puzzle. He would only pause for the coffee breaks, entertaining Sarah while I fetched cookies from the kitchen. Later in the evening, Sarah would gather her clippings and papers in a corner, stuff them into her bag, and head home.

'Turn on the light, please! How many times do I have to tell you? I can't sleep with the lights off!' I shouted.

'Give me a few more minutes, I'm testing something here,' Julien replied.

'Right … what is it this time?' I murmured in irritation.

'The speed of darkness.'

Julien was like my father. They could spend hours together in the basement trying out new ideas, new projects. They all started with good intentions, but never really got anywhere. Not that it mattered to them. It was the experiment that counted, not the results.

'Darkness does not move! Can you please turn the light on, now?' Julien left the bedroom, full of resentment.

Darkness does not move. It stays still. Light is its killer: it does the deed quickly and painlessly. Does liking the light make you complicit in the murder of darkness and younger brothers' experiments? Maybe I really was a killer. An unconscious one, but guilty nonetheless. I had no right to shout at him. He missed our father as much as I did; and maybe more. I turned on the light and fell asleep.

☼

On a late spring evening, Sarah and I decided to enjoy the final rays of sunshine, and a handful of *Trappiste* beers, at Parc Cinquantenaire. By then she had become as constant in my life as the morning bus ride through the heart of Matongé, and the raindrops that flowed down the windows to blur the vivid colours of the African shops outside.

'What was your mother like?' I dared to ask.

'I don't know. I don't really have any memories of her. She left soon after I turned four.'

'Don't you ever talk about her with your father?'

'Not really. He's too busy with his job and the constant moving around. We rarely talk about anything.'

She lay down on the grass and closed her eyes. I sipped a cold Chimay Bleu and kept my eyes trained on her. *Le fils de l'homme* by Magritte came to my mind; there everything we see hides other things in fresh layers of secrecy. With Sarah it was the same. The mystery she spun around her life spun itself around me as well. I was captive.

'A woman knows what another woman wants, right?' she asked suddenly.

'I guess so ...'

'Do you know what I want?'

I never really got to know what was on Sarah's mind. She enjoyed asking questions, but never giving answers. She had secrets I wanted to know. Secrets I had to know. Her charm was all tied up in that, in what she left unsaid.

Around us, a group of girls were planning their summer holidays while waiting for a football match to end.

'How about Morocco?' one suggested.

'Too hot ... let's go to Barcelona. A bit of paella, a bit of beach. Perfect combination,' another replied.

Further down, a man lit up a cigarette and reabsorbed himself in his book. Sarah got up and leaned over. Her green eyes close to mine. Her right hand on mine.

'We should do the same,' she said.

'What do you mean?'

'Stop living in our dream-world, paintings and all that stuff. We should just go for simple, foolish pleasures like everyone else. Did you hear those girls? Beach and paella, that's what they really want ... maybe we should be more like that, you know, just do what we want and see what it feels like ...'

The sky turned slowly orange and a soft breeze started blowing. Sarah came closer; she shivered and folded her arms. Soon enough, the girls and the man had left us alone. Sarah's green eyes were inches away from mine, dipping in and out of them. I blushed and looked down. She touched my hair. A moment afterwards, she was kissing me. I hesitated at first, and then I kissed her back. The cool breeze subsided. Below us, the wet ground trembled as the metro passed between Merode and Schuman. I breathed heavily. Minutes ran by. Everything around us moved, turned and changed.

Was that what I wanted? I wasn't sure. I fell silent and dreamy. Fantasy had become a dramatic reality, like in Chagall's paintings. A single colour can define our meaning in life, and that is the colour of love, he believed. At last, the sun drowned in a flaming orange sky, revealing the city, and my love for all that it promised.

☼

The next day, Julien and I met Sarah for a coffee at Ultime-atome, her favourite bar in Place Saint Boniface. Julien spotted her arms waving from a secluded booth at the back of the room. Sarah had dedicated the whole morning to her end-of-year project: designing a logo for a start-up social network.

'Julien! It's been too long!' She got up to greet him with an affectionate hug, and I hung back. Then came my turn. I could not move. I tried, but I was motionless. I blushed. Sarah stepped forward, embraced me and gently kissed my left cheek. 'Salut chérie,' she said.

I smiled and felt tenderness envelop me. I was not sure how far it stretched. Maybe it took in the whole city. Maybe just the three of us.

'So Julien, how are you? What have you been up to?' Sarah asked.

'Have you ever noticed all those men playing cards in the park?' he replied.

'Yeah, I guess so. What about them?'

'I've placed them under observation.'

'What do you mean under observation?' she smiled; Julien always charmed her with his peculiarities.

'Well, I'm observing their behaviour. You know, tracking all their movements: at what time they meet, how long a single game lasts, how many words they speak to each other. Take a look; I've recorded everything in this notebook. It's interesting.'

'That's how you spend your afternoons? Okaaaay ... Come and see my logo. What do you think?'

'It's nice! The colours are a bit brash though.'

'You think?'

Sarah looked at me but I just shrugged. Julien's hot chocolate and my *lait russe* arrived. I sipped slowly from it.

'Hey Anaïs, do you think that milk is really from Russia?' Julien asked, penetrating my silence.

Sarah laughed; I smiled. To that question, like so many others running through my head, I had no answer.

Back home, Julien could not contain his curiosity.

'So, what's going on between you and Sarah?'

'What do you mean?'

157

'Come on, don't lie to me. You know that I know,' he uttered.

Of course he knew. Julien could read me so easily. There was no need to say it. Still, I felt uneasy talking about the previous night with Sarah. Was I ashamed? Yes, but it was my secret this time. Was I happy? Yes, but I didn't want to share it. Was I confused? Yes, but nobody had to know. Not even Julien. I turned on the light and he disappeared into the living room. As usual. I wish I could do that whenever people make me claustrophobic.

☼

I have no memory of the following weeks of seminars. What did we talk about? What did we learn? None of it mattered a damn because Sarah was missing. I didn't see her at university. She wasn't at the art gallery in the evening. She didn't return my calls. Did she exist at all?

I asked other classmates. None had seen her. None had really noticed her absence, they admitted. They had all loved her at first, chatty and funny as she was, but then found her too weird to be considered a friend.

Nobody can be too weird for a city like Brussels, I had thought. That's what I loved about the place. That's what I loved about Sarah. Her weirdness was addictive. Like Julien's. I hadn't heard from him either since he had left to visit mum for a 'few days'. It had been longer than that. And I missed him, especially at night.

I lay down on my bed and looked up at the ceiling. In the middle, a poster of *Blue Sky*, by Kandinsky. Sarah had given it to me as a present for my twenty-fifth birthday, just a month before. 'The blazing blue in the background evokes the freedom to dream,' she had read from the description card. I didn't feel any freedom or willingness to dream at all. The blue sky, inside and outside my room, only reminded me of my isolation.

There I was, in my solitude, once again. Probably the place I knew best.

☼

Brussels is the city of easy friendship, I've heard many times. You meet someone, you chat for a few minutes, and suddenly you are with a new friend. Sarah had been my only friend for months and now that she was missing, I felt lost. Even so, Brussels seemed to be the perfect place to overcome that feeling. One night, on my way home, I ended up at a house full of strangers. As I was walking up the stairs I asked myself if what I was doing was not wholly pathetic. But it only took a few minutes before I realised that crashing parties was the most *Bruxellois* thing that a foreigner could do.

What's your name?

Where are you from?

How long are you going to stay?

As if the answers to all of those questions really mattered. Soon nothing really mattered anyway, words and names vanishing in beer and laughter.

At times, too much alcohol would lead to headaches and nightmares. When I awoke in the middle of the night, he was there, beside me. *I've done it again*, I thought, staring at his sleeping face on the pillow. I had a quick look at my mobile phone: still no messages. The night was about to meet the new day in a white sky. They say white is the colour of purity. Sadly, I noticed my red underwear.

Back home I had never realised how easy getting somebody into bed could be. I wasn't interested before, until the point I felt the need to fill emptiness with foolish reality. In my bed, a melting pot of young international-minded bodies, one after another, different in origin and attitude. Green eyes, like Sarah's, were all they had in common. All they had to have in common. I never loved any of them nor they me. I looked again at my red underwear. Red is the colour of excitement, guilt, pain, passion, blood and anger.

Suddenly, he opened his eyes. I touched his hair. He smiled. I smiled back and said it was time for him to go.

☼

'Meet me at Parking 58. Usual time. S.' After three weeks of silence Sarah had finally reappeared with a text message.

She was late. As if meticulously planned in advance, her delays always allowed me to get into the mind-set needed to meet her wild green eyes, her questions, her self. Parking 58 was a peculiar parking area on top of a ten floor building in the centre of town. In late spring, as soon as the temperature rose, we'd get lost up there just to get a breath of fresh air. It's where Sarah once confessed how much she missed not having a sister.

'I envy you for having Julien.'

'You do?'

'Sure, it's nice to have someone so close. I always wanted to have an older sister, who understands your needs and who'd answer all your questions ...'

'Like what?'

'Like ... I don't know, like ... how to apply nail polish.'

'Julien doesn't know how to apply nail polish!'

She had laughed hysterically.

Now I was back there again, ten storeys up, the Grand-Place tower dominating the skyline in front of me. Further down, the Palais de Justice, with its monumental golden dome, looked impenetrable. I leaned over the parapet. The Delhaize on the corner was shutting its doors; a man was jogging along the pavement with his dog; cars were temporarily piling up at the traffic light before speeding off as the light turned green. Finally, I heard slow, regular footsteps. I felt her standing close, I didn't dare move. What would I tell her? What would she tell me? Did I want to be there at all?

'Anaïs,' she called, and I turned, hypnotised. In the darkness of the rooftop, I couldn't see much of her, though I felt overwhelmed by the presence of her body in front of me.

She wasn't a dream. She was real and fragile. All those thoughts and doubts from the weeks gone by, they all vanished. I wanted to tell her how much I had been thinking of her. How I had slept with random guys in the hope of evoking that night in the park … This and much more, I wanted to tell her.

'What's up Sarah?' I asked instead.

'I'm sorry; I had to go away for a while.'

'Where to?'

She hugged me. 'Can you feel me?'

I held her, aware that she had something important to share.

Nine months have passed since that rainy November afternoon when I first met Sarah. It still rains a lot. Tonight at Parking 58 is Sarah's last night. Her dad is moving again.

'Follow me,' she commands.

I fall silent, like that night when she first touched me. Julien once told me that a woman can speak as many as ten thousand words per day. I wonder how many can be thought. Right now, I have no words to say, but a million words to think. If only we could go back to the beginning. The unusual conversations at the art gallery; the long walks by the dirty canal; the spring evenings at the park. I still want to lay down at sunset with her. I still want to feel her body close to mine, like now at Parking 58. But to follow implies the future, the unknown. Sarah's place in it is somehow incomplete. My own place in it is not yet defined. It's too early. I can see the disappointment in her eyes.

'We are allowed to be foolish,' she had said. What should I do? I begin to see a new image of life, timeless and dreamy, without solemn pledges. A new picture, tempting in its simplicity but frightening in its implications. How could I explain my escape from reality?

Night gives way to early morning. When I wake I find myself alone but still on the roof of Parking 58. I must have drifted from thoughts into sleep. Was I dreaming? Maybe. Nothing around reminds me of the night before with her. Empty cans – Sarah doesn't drink from cans. Cigarette butts – Sarah doesn't smoke. A note on the floor – Sarah doesn't like writing.

Emptiness.

On the left, at the top: a point.

On the right, at the bottom: another point.

And in the middle nothing.

And nothing is a lot, really.

Anyway, it's more than something.

The words on the note are Kandinsky's. Beside the note, a silver coin. Kandinsky wasn't random. He believed that colours had meanings. Like Sarah and I did. Can colours really help us understand life? Maybe they do. Colours describe words, objects, people. Sarah used to believe that life was a white canvas to be painted by individuals. For some people it's a big wide canvas with its delights and disappointments. For others it's a small one: they paint so fast that they run out of colours and all of a sudden their canvas is finished. Some people have the ambition to produce a truly great work, but are disillusioned by the outcome and destroy the canvas rather than starting over. These paintings are never offered any official ceremony when entering the after-canvas world.

No song, no celebration, no applause.

A silver-grey coin, the neutral land. A call for choice. I flip it in the air.

The streets are empty on Sunday mornings. And there I am, walking home, alone. Around me, old *maisons de maître*, colourful bars, grey offices. I can smell the dark roasted malt beers, the yellow French fries, the sweetness of hot chocolate.

Sarah left and my silence didn't stop her. 'Follow me,' she had asked. Then a silver coin, heads or tails, black or white. Black, the final answer. Black, the absence of all colours. Black, the silence. My silence back to Sarah. My goodbye to the past. With no celebration. My canvas–world is now here, in this city. I could not leave it. Finally, I can sleep with the lights off. The darkness does not scare me anymore. Julien has moved back home, and my childhood has disappeared beneath him. My stories are my brushes, each one brandishing its own colour. Yellow energy, green harmony, blue nostalgia, red passion, orange love, black silence. Between the gaps, the magic and memory of Parking 58 and the rain–swept sky beyond.

ABOUT THE AUTHORS

The nine authors are members of the Brussels Creative Writers. Since its foundation in early 2008, the group meets on a weekly basis to write stories on the spot and exchange feedback on each other's work. The group also organises workshops for the wider public.

*Contact: **info@themeantime.be***

 Olivier Gbezera is currently working on his first collection of short stories. Born in Ghent, Belgium, after living in the United States, the Central African Republic, France and Italy, he settled down in Brussels in 2006.

 Edina Dóci is a co-founder and coordinator of the Brussels Creative Writers, and facilitator of writing workshops. She is currently working towards a PhD in psychology. Originally from Budapest, Hungary, she has lived in Brussels since 2007.

Alfredo Zucchi, Italian, won the *Sea of words 2010* writing competition with his short story *Milena is a sex-bomb*. He also wrote and directed the play *Mozart - tale of an expat*, performed at Bozar, Brussels, in June 2010. He is now based in Barcelona, having lived in Brussels from 2007-2010.

Monica Westerén, from Finland, is a co-founder and coordinator of the Brussels Creative Writers as well as organiser and facilitator of creative writing workshops. She studied Comparative Literature and has experience in journalism and travel writing. She has lived in Brussels since 2008.

Nick Jacobs, British-American, is a French and Spanish literature graduate who has lived in Brussels since 2008. His published journalistic work ranges from film and music reviews to political blogs and opinion pieces. Political satire is a major inspiration for his fictional work.

Sybille Regout, Belgian, was a finalist in the 1999 *Prix littéraire Victor Rossel des jeunes* writing competition. She is now working towards a PhD in Social Sciences and lives in Kraainem, Brussels.

Dany G. Zuwen (born Gaston Ndanyuzwe) is the author of the 2010 science fiction novel *Tenebrae – Mantax*. He received an honourable mention for his short story *Poor Man's Freedom* in the 2010 *Lorian Hemingway competition*. Dany was born in Gitarama, Rwanda. He landed in Belgium in 1995, and has been living in Brussels ever since.

Enrique Medarde, Spanish, is an amateur writer who has penned poems, comic book scripts and other short stories. He is currently working on a cook book and maintains a cooking blog. Originally from Salamanca, he has lived in Brussels for four years.

Ylenia Maitino, Italian, is the author of *Domani il buio non esiste*, a poetry collection published in 2007. She is currently working on a photography-poetry book. She first arrived in Brussels in 2005.

Many thanks to Myra Bernardi and Sophie Freeman for their help in proofreading the collection.

The Meantime was published in Brussels in July 2012.

Made in the USA
Charleston, SC
26 September 2012